Praise for SHERI REYNOLDS

"Ms. Reynolds's poetic gifts are uncommonly powerful."
—*The New York Times*

"Reynolds is a wonderful storyteller and master of pastoral imagery."
—*The New York Times Book Review*

"Reynolds . . . is a gifted writer with a deceptively simple style and a keen ear for dialogue." —*The Boston Globe*

"Reynolds is the newest and most exciting voice to emerge in contemporary southern fiction." —*San Francisco Bay Guardian*

"[A]s true as butter in your grits. . . . [a] powerful drama with pathos, poetry, and, unexpectedly, hope."
—*People* magazine, for *The Sweet In-Between*

"[A] sweet coming-of-age story, thanks to its young, wise-beyond-her-years, Scout Finch-esque heroine."
—*Entertainment Weekly,* for *The Sweet In-Between*

The Sweet
IN-BETWEEN

The Sweet

IN-BETWEEN

SHERI REYNOLDS

TURNER

Turner Publishing Company

4507 Charlotte Avenue • Suite 100 • Nashville, Tennessee 37209

www.turnerpublishing.com

Cover design by Beth Middleworth
Book design by Glen Edelstein

Library of Congress Cataloging-in-Publication Data

Reynolds, Sheri.
 The sweet in-between / Sheri Reynolds.
   p. cm.
 ISBN 978-1-61858-033-7 (pbk)
1. Teenage girls--Fiction. 2. Gender identity--Fiction. 3. Domestic fiction. I. Title.
PS3568.E8975R43 2012
813'.54--dc23
                    2012023055

For BARBARA M. BROWN

Acknowledgements

I AM DEEPLY GRATEFUL FOR THE INSIGHTS provided by my readers: Chritin Lore Weber, Barbara Brown, Jenean Hall, Amy Tudor, Andrew Follmer, and Janet Peery. I also want to thank Candice Fuhrman, my agent, and Shaye Areheart, my editor, for their careful work on this manuscript.

The Sweet
IN-BETWEEN

Part ONE

WE'VE COME OUT HERE TO FISH, me and Quincy and Daphne and Aunt Glo. Daphne's got her lunch box filled with rotten chicken necks, the rottener the better for the crabs. So I move upwind, past the stench. I've got my daddy's old rod and reel, the red one with the soft cork handle. It's got dents from where his fingers used to go.

It's September now, and we've come out here to fish. But Quincy brought his skateboard, and he's riding it all the way to the end of the pier, pissing off the heron who was catching a nap. Quincy's wheels thrum-drum through the cracks between boards, and that heron stretches out and takes off. If I could fly like that, I wouldn't even mind looking so prehistoric. The heron settles on a channel marker out there in the bay and pulls his head into his shoulders like somebody cold.

Aunt Glo helps Daphne tie her chicken necks with string and dangle them down into the Water. Daphne sniffs her fingers and says, "Ugh," but she must like the smell, the way she sniffs them over and over. "Ugh," she says and scrunches up her nose.

I've got my own cooler, and stashed inside it there's a can of soda, a pack of saltines, a plastic bag with my still-frozen squid, and an army knife sharp enough to cut it. So I dig out a piece of squid and saw it right there, add my slashes to the thousand already carved into this wood. I choose a good-size hunk, the head, and hook it to my line. I hook it three times, through the flesh and through the eye, blackjuice squirting out at me, and when I cast, my line zings high and plops hard in the bay.

Now it's the wait, the knock-knock of the line and deciding whether it's a crab or something bigger, the reeling in sometimes, the breeze on my face, my face in the sun. It's September, but the sun's still hot, and when I close my eyes, I can pretend I'm on a boat sailing off to somewhere else.

On that boat, heading north with my face in the wind, I can forget the sounds I heard last night: the banging around, the giggles and high-pitched "shit!"s I thought at first it was just a dream and those girls were at *my* door and making fun of *me*. It was late in the night, and when I woke up, I figured somebody was pulling a prank on old Jarvis Stanley right next door.

But that was yesterday.

With the water slapping soft against the wood, I pretend I'm a tugboat captain, pulling a barge loaded with gold all the way up to Annapolis, and I wonder if barges ever carry anything besides gravel or coal, if barges go to Annapolis at all. Annapolis is the farthest I've ever been, but someday I'll go farther. I'll go someplace where crazy things don't happen, where girls don't die like that girl died last night, right there in Jarvis Stanley's living room.

Today I plan to catch a flounder. Maybe two.

THIS MORNING WHEN THE SCHOOL BUS CAME, we were all in our pajamas. Aunt Glo said, "Well, I swannee," and waved the driver on. Weren't none of us ready, not even me, and I've always got my book bag packed and sitting by the door.

Aunt Glo made us jelly toast and sat there looking at the jelly knife for the longest time and shaking her head, and I couldn't stop thinking how jelly tastes sweet but blood does not. When I saw that dead girl, I bit my lip and didn't even know it until I swallowed. My blood went down, her blood ran out, in the grooves of the floorboards behind Jarvis Stanley's couch where she fell.

We didn't get much sleep.

It was four in the morning, and the banging came first, then the giggling, then the sound I found out later was a window forced up. Then there was the hot sound, a shotgun cracking. And after that, the screaming, or maybe the screaming started at the exact same time. Then the galloping, but that was really us—all running down the stairs, and by then we were all right there, me and Quincy peeking out the window, and Aunt Glo on the phone with 911, Daphne crying hard as she could squall and her not even knowing yet what was going on. Then the other girl screaming and beating on *our* door. Then the police sirens, and the ambulance, and that other girl shivering and crouching on our porch, on our side of the duplex, till Aunt Glo finally let her in.

Y OU GOT A BITE," Quincy says. He scares me, and I jump. Sure enough, my pole tip's kicking. I reel it in, but it's too late. My bait's gone.

"How come you're not fishing?" I ask him. He's got a newer rod and reel than me.

He shrugs. "Later," he says and skates away like everything's fine, like this day's ordinary as butter in your grits.

I keep wishing for an ordinary day, but my stomach's murky and sloshing around, and it feels like I've got little fish chomping at my guts. Even though the pier's not really pitching, I'm queasy and can't watch the water long.

So I go over to check on Daphne and Aunt Glo. Aunt Glo's got her sunglasses on, and she's leaned back in her beach chair, so I can't tell if she's awake or not. Daphne says, "Smell my fingers," and shoves them toward my nose, but I slap her grubby hand away.

"Piss-head," she says, pouting, and turns back to her string, teasing it up from the water, trying to hold on to the crab.

"Aunt Glo," I say, "I'm going for a walk," but Aunt Glo doesn't move. "Aunt Glo," I repeat. "I'll be back in a little bit."

And since she doesn't stop me, I take off.

I WALK ALONG THE BEACH AWHILE. It's better when I'm walking. The tide's falling, and there's black seaweed along the edges where water used to be. It looks like the stuff inside a cassette tape, pulled out and curling all around itself I think of all the tapes my daddy used to have, tapes his old girlfriends made. They said things like "For Greg. Play when lonely or sad" or "To Greg, on our two-month anniversary." He kept them in the console of his truck, and when we moved up here, we listened to those songs all the way from Georgia to Virginia. But one night when Daddy and Aunt Glo got in a bad love spat, she tore out all the tapes and left them wadded on the floorboards, the plastic cases cracked from where she smashed them.

I kick through the seaweed with my sneakers.

After a while, Quincy comes up, skateboard under his arm, saying, "Looka here," and he shows me the caps from tire stems in his pocket, the little black hoods he's unscrewed. It's his favorite hobby, next to skateboarding, stealing tire-stem caps. I don't know why he does it. He has a whole sockful back at the house.

"Whose are they?" I ask, but he doesn't know. He tells me he's going to the post office, but what he means is he's going to the parking lot behind it where he's built a ramp out of an old piece of plywood leaned against the delivery dock. They opened a new post office last year, a big one out on the highway. They boarded up the windows of the old one with signs that say FOR LEASE OR SALE.

"What about Aunt Glo?" I ask him.

"What about her?" Quincy says and grins. He's Aunt Glo's baby son and gets away with a lot. He's got stringy hair that needs cutting, hanging in his eyes, and a deep one-sided dimple that makes him look like he thinks the whole world's retarded, even though I know better.

Last night he got ahold of my T-shirt when they took that girl away. They put her on a stretcher and rolled her through the porch light, the covers all bloodied from where they pulled them over her head. Quincy nearly strangled me, twisting my shirt so hard. I had to elbow him to make him quit. Quincy's twelve, but he looks ten.

I tell him, "Aunt Glo'll be pissed if you sneak off to the PO without asking."

"She won't even know it," Quincy claims. "She popped an Oxy 'fore we left. She's probably snoring by now. Scaring off all Daphne's crabs. You coming?"

"Nah," I say. "I better go check on 'em."

"Whatever," Quincy says, but he's dragging as he crosses all that sand. I can tell he doesn't want to skate any more than I want to fish. But sometimes you have to pass a day—in one way or another—just to get to tomorrow.

Back on the dock, Daphne's pulled up a crab, and she's squealing as she tries to catch it in her net. It drops into the water before I can help her. "It's the third time that shit-sucker fell off," she whines.

Aunt Glo's not asleep after all, 'cause she says, "Girl, you better watch your language," but there's no threat in her voice. It's like all her energy's leeched out, and I feel sorry for Aunt Glo, having to put up with so much. Aunt Glo's oldest boy, Tim-Tim, taught Daphne to cuss back before she even lost her baby lisp. Now she's seven and a half and set in her ways. There's nothing any of us can do about it. "I'm gone blister your hide," Aunt Glo adds.

Daphne mocks her, mouthing back her words, but without making any sounds. Aunt Glo doesn't see it. She's still lost behind her sunglasses, and I wonder if she's picturing Jarvis Stanley and how crazy he looked, just woke up and whiskery, waving that shotgun around, saying, "I thought they was burglers" and through my winder for?" Even after the police arrived, Jarvis kept saying, "Anybody breaks in my house in the middle of the night *deserves* to get shot."

But then there was that other girl, the screaming one, who waved around a piece of paper, saying, "We rented it. We paid!"

MY SQUID'S THAWED OUT AND EASIER TO CUT, so I chop up two great hunks and put one on either hook. Maybe I'll get lucky and catch that flounder. If I catch flounder, I won't tell, and I won't share it, either. I'll fill my cooler with croakers and put them on the top, and while Aunt Glo fries them up, I'll sneak back to the beach and build a fire and eat the flounder by myself. I make these kinds of plans while I fish.

Those two girls were the first to arrive, but supposedly, two more were coming. Somebody must have called them—maybe the police. They'd all graduated from the same school a few years back, and they were getting together to celebrate. The crying girl had recently gotten engaged. She showed us all her tiny diamond. The dead girl was supposed to be a bridesmaid. They had catalogs to pick out dresses and matching shoes. I sat with the crying girl on our striped couch while the police asked her questions. She thanked me for the blanket I put over her legs and didn't notice it had a stain from where somebody had dropped some Chef Boyardee. Once she asked me for some water, and when she took the cup, she used two hands. Both of them trembled. So I sat close by in case she needed anything else, and I watched as she showed the policeman their rental agreement again and again. Her name was Rhonda.

They'd rented the house for a five-night getaway, two blocks from the water. Sure enough, it gave Jarvis Stanley's address,

206-A Osprey Lane, right next door to us at 206-B. But the only vacation rental on our block—probably the only vacation rental in the whole town—was at 207, across the street. This isn't the sort of place people come for vacation unless they're fishermen or biologists studying currents or horseshoe crabs. Just because a place is on a body of water doesn't make it a resort. But maybe those girls didn't know it. Maybe they rented over the Internet or something.

They thought they'd been locked out. The rental agent said the key would be under a fern on the doorstep, but there wasn't a fern at all. They knocked and banged, like that would help, and when they saw a window they could open, they decided to climb inside it. They'd paid for the place, and there was nobody to call, not till morning, anyway. They'd been driving since they got off work from way down near Atlanta, and they had the paper right there, the girl waved it around, and it proved they had the right.

Jarvis Stanley woke up to intruders in his house, bumping in the dark, not even trying to be quiet. "Sounded like a bulldozer," he said. He'd been robbed the year before, lost his television set, so he didn't hesitate to shoot that gun, and he had pretty good aim for such an old fellow without his glasses. Who knows why he didn't kill the other girl? Maybe she hit the light switch right that second. Maybe when he saw her there with her ponytail up high on her head, he figured out they weren't just your run-of-the-mill robbers.

On Aunt Glo's couch, that girl smelled strong, not like perfume but like something else, maybe peppers. I had a feeling she'd never smelled that way before in all her life, and I thought the smell might be a private one. It made my guts ache. It made me want to pull her head into my lap and rub it like a baby bunny. Rhonda. You could tell how pretty she'd be if her nose weren't red and running and her mascara all smeared around.

THERE'S NO CONFUSION BETWEEN a crab and a drum. Crabs peck at your line, but when you move it, most times they fall right off. When a red drum hits, and the line clenches tight, and the rod starts to bow, it yanks you right out of your thoughts, and nothing matters but your hands.

My hands wheel in that line, over slow and under fast, and I'm still hoping it's a flounder and hoping my reel doesn't lock. But when it comes in closer, I holler to Daphne to come with the net 'cause I can tell from how it moves in the water that it's thicker than flounder. And then I see that I've got two, fighting opposite hooks.

Daphne's jumping and giggling, waiting with the net. She lays down on her belly and holds the net as far as she can reach. But there's no danger of losing these fish. One has swallowed the hook, and it takes almost as long to rip out the other one. Aunt Glo comes to help, pulls a rag out her pocket and holds the fish so it won't fin her while she works. "Oooh, them's pretty," she says. "Wish I had a camera! Get a picture of you holding 'em and send it to your daddy!"

Then a funny look crosses her face, and I know that in another way, she's glad she left her camera at home.

Red drum have spots on either side of their tails, big black blotches. This year they're endangered and have to be eighteen inches to keep. I can't remember how long they had to be last year. My two are thirteen and fourteen inches, but there's no chance in hell we're throwing them back. They're supper, and besides that, no game warden around is gonna check our cooler today. It'd be a sorry thing to do to people who witnessed a tragedy like we did last night.

"Rig me a pole," Daphne says. "I'm gonna catch some, too."

So I cut her some bait and fix up Quincy's pole. "What about your crabs?"

"I'll get 'em later," she says.

Daphne's not bad at casting. She comes fishing with me most Sunday afternoons, so she's had some practice. But her line doesn't go out too far in the harbor. She's short, with a little fat belly that perches on the elastic in her shorts. No matter what shirt she wears, you can always see her belly button through it. She was born too early—to Aunt Glo's daughter Constance, who didn't tell anybody she was having a baby until the day she went into labor. So Daphne stayed in the hospital a long time. She's still got scars from where they put the tubes in her, and all her grades in school are NIs for "needs improvement."

As soon as Daphne's hook hits bottom, the red drum strikes. She squeals and starts reeling, but it's too much, and soon she's saying, "Help me!" then screaming, "Grammy!" and Aunt Glo reels it in until the very end, when Daphne pulls it out so she can lay official claim.

It's a big one, but not big enough. We put it in the cooler with the others. It's like playing dominoes, laying those black spots on top of one another.

Daphne's got long inky-looking hair that would drive me crazy if it grew on my head, falling in my face and dipping in my squid every time I leaned over to sliver off a piece. Aunt Glo baits Daphne's hook again 'cause I'm busy pulling in another red drum. There's a school of 'em running right through this harbor and nobody but us to partake.

Even though we're cheering and laughing and hauling in fish, I can't help thinking about those girls, wondering if we'd have met them, wondering if they'd be sitting on the beach right now, rubbing suntan lotion on each other, if Jarvis Stanley hadn't ruined their vacation.

Even though I don't like Jarvis Stanley and I hope he rots in hell, I feel a little bit sorry that he killed a girl by accident. It must have scared him bad, for him to shoot her. Then another part of me's glad a girl finally got the best of him, even if she had to die to do it.

I ask Aunt Glo, "You reckon Jarvis Stanley'll go to prison?"

"No," she says. "But that rental lady might."

I hadn't thought about the rental lady being accountable. It was a bad mistake to make, no question, but I like the rental lady and don't want her to get in trouble. She's paid me ten dollars a week to cut her grass ever since she fixed up that house.

"Is the women's prison the same place as the men's?" I ask.

"No," Aunt Glo says. "Good thing, too." Then she snorts and says, 'Your daddy'd see it different. I'll warrant you that." And after that I can't stop picturing my daddy and the vacation-rental lady living together in prison, sharing a cell, him doing time for possession with intention to distribute, and her doing time for what? A typo?

In a while, we have enough fish for supper three times over. We'll freeze the extras and eat red drum so many nights in a row that pretty soon we'll be craving frozen pizza again.

The squid has slicked up on my fingers, sticky and clear like glue, and my fingernails shine in the afternoon sun. I scrape off the squid grease so nobody'll think I painted my fingernails. That's just the sort of thing Quincy'd tease me about.

Maybe Aunt Glo reads my thoughts, 'cause she asks, "Where's Quin?"

"Post office," I say.

"I thought he was restricted," she says. "Weren't he restricted?"

"That was last week," I tell her.

"Oh," she says. She gets confused like this sometimes, but I try to keep her straight.

When we get back to the house, Quincy's there, and so is Tim-Tim. He still lives at home but usually sleeps at his girlfriend's. He dropped out of school a couple of years back and cleans people's heating units now.

"Help us gut these fish," Aunt Glo says, but Quincy and Tim-Tim ignore her. They're playing at the Xbox, trying to kill each other off with fire and arrows.

"I'll do it," I say, because I love Aunt Glo, and besides that, Quincy and Tim-Tim don't have to listen to her. She's their momma, and she'll stick with them no matter what. Me—I have to work for her affection. She's not really even my aunt.

"Thank you, baby," she says, and I take the fish out to the backyard to clean. It'd be easier to do it on the front porch, where the water hose is, but I don't want to be out front. That dead girl's car is still parked there, not twenty feet from our doorstep, and even though I didn't know her, I can't stand to look at her car, just sitting there like that.

Turns out I can't stand to be indoors, either, so after supper, I follow Tim-Tim and Quincy down to the corner and back behind the old post office. I keep replaying the night before and wish I'd saved up enough money to check in to the Holiday Inn for the rest of my life. Aunt Glo used to clean rooms there and swore that rats came up through the plumbing and swam around in the commodes, but I wouldn't even care. I'd put a brick on my commode lid and sleep fine.

Behind the post office, the older boys are throwing quarters up against the bricks and seeing whose money snuggles closest to the wall. Closest quarter wins the lot—and I've got quarters in my pocket, a whole bunch of them, but I know better than to ask in on the game.

I squat by the sidelines and keep quiet. As long as I'm with Tim-Tim, they'll let me stay.

"Did you see her?" one boy asks. "After she was dead?"

"Yeah," Tim-Tim says, even though he wasn't there. "It was—" He shakes his head, like it was indescribable.

"Was she pretty?" somebody asks.

"Not after he shot her," Tim-Tim says, and everybody laughs, and I feel hot around my collar and hot all through my face. I pull down my ball cap so nobody will look at me. But they all do.

"Did you see her, too?" this boy named Rick asks. I've known him a long time and even had to sit next to him in algebra last year. "Hey, *Kendra*," he says, "did you see that dead girl?" I look down at the pieces of gravel in the parking lot and imagine picking one up, the pointiest one I can find, and throwing it right between his eyes.

"He asked you a question," Tim-Tim says. "Don't be a pussy." They all laugh at that.

"Yeah," I whisper. "I saw her."

So I wait until they've started their next round of the game, until they're busy talking about Jarvis Stanley and what's gonna happen to him, and then I slip off.

I'd walk to the pier if it wasn't so dark. Most times the night doesn't bother me, but tonight I keep mistaking shadows for things they're not. When wind hits the pampas grass outside Miss Mattie's and makes the tall stalks sway, I think for sure something's in there, and it's not until I'm across the street that I remember we don't have panthers or mountain lions either one in town.

I'd walk to the carnival grounds, where I go sometimes, but it seems too far away and like my legs might give out before I get there. Maybe it's because I didn't get enough sleep, but I feel funny, like I might not be who I always thought, like I might be a robot, or I might be walking around inside a comic book and not even know it.

WHEN I GET HOME, Daphne's on the couch with Aunt Glo, watching a crime show on TV They're cuddled up under a sheet, and Daphne says, "Would they put Kenny in the boy's prison or the girl's?" and Aunt Glo says, "Kenny's not going to prison! Not never!" And she smiles at me so sweet.

"'Night," I say, and they tell me good night, and then I go up to the room I share with Daphne, and I tighten the ACE bandage I've got strapped around my chest. I don't look when I do it. I can't stand to see them, so big and squishy. I hate them more than anything. I wrap myself as tight as I can stand it and hope my tits will turn black like an old stumped toenail and fall off in my sleep.

I GET UP AT TWO, like I do every night, climb down from the top bunk, careful, trying not to squeak the ladder or shake the bed and wake up Daphne, who sleeps on the bottom. I go to the bathroom and drink as much water as I can hold. Sometimes I don't even remember doing it. I just wake up on the can, sitting there drinking from my blue plastic cup. It's a great big cup I got from the state fair the year I was twelve, the last year we went, because Daddy went to prison after that, and Aunt Glo can't manage all us heathens in the city by herself. Every night I fill my cup and drain it twice before I go back to sleep. It's like a challenge—and I do it for my body because I know it needs the water.

That way, when I wake up at six, I use the bathroom, and I'm done with it. I don't drink hardly anything with my breakfast, just the tiniest sips, and I'm careful when I brush my teeth to spit everything back out, so at school, I won't have to go. There's no place on earth I dread worse than the girls' bathroom. So far this year, I haven't had to use it.

But tonight I can't swallow. It's like something's in my throat, even though look in the mirror and don't see a thing except tonsils. It takes forever to get one glass of water down.

Last night this time, those two girls were still driving. They were probably laughing, playing their music—maybe they were picking out wedding songs—and slurping the last bits of Coca-Cola from their cups.

If I'd known to stay awake when I got up to drink, if I'd gone to sit on the porch like I sometimes do, I could have stopped what happened next. I could have told them they were at the wrong house and pointed them across the street where the fern sat on the house key and nobody inside had a gun.

I force down water, gulping and burping and gulping some more.

Then I hear something bang around outside, and I'm not sure if I'm making it up, maybe replaying noises from last night. I turn out the light and peek out the bathroom window, hoping it's wind. But Tim-Tim's got his girlfriend bent over the hood of that dead girl's Pontiac, and what I'm hearing is his hip bones slapping against her backside, her hip bones drumming against that red car, both of them groaning, and for the second time in two nights, I'm looking out the window at something I know I shouldn't see.

So I finish my water and go back to bed. But I've got a rhyme in my head that won't let me sleep. *Red drum running, red drum strumming.* I say it over and over, picturing that dead girl's car and hearing the sounds of hips hitting metal long after they must be through. In my mind, that dead girl turns into a fish, a red drum, and Tim-Tim's girlfriend—she's a red drum, too. Then I'm a fish with them, swimming right behind, my eyes and mouth wide open, water rushing inside me but flowing back out through my gills.

I have never been so thirsty in all my life.

A LL NIGHT I'M TOO CRANKED UP TO SLEEP. Then I get on the bus and can't hardly stay awake, and I don't turn around even when Darren Cannon shoots rubber bands at the back of my head. I lean against the window and breathe in the smells of erasers and oily vinyl and diesel as we jerk from stop to stop.

When I get to school, I walk straight through the Commons Area, fast and quiet with my face held down, and hope nobody will see me. I tell the hall monitor I'm going to Morning Devotional, like always, and he lets me into the classroom where the Christian athletes hold prayers before school.

I'm not much of an athlete, or much of a Christian, but I go there every day because nobody throws me out. My friend Wendy Honeycutt's there. She's a frog-eyed girl with long blond hair that she rolls on hot rollers and pulls back in a headband that matches her blouse. I've known her since we were both in Girl Scouts. For a long time, Aunt Glo had a picture of us on the refrigerator. We'd done a bike-a-thon to raise money for cancer or diabetes or something, and me and Wendy were waving from our bikes.

Daddy and Aunt Glo got me that bike for the occasion. Before that, I'd ridden Tim-Tim's sometimes, and before that, when I was really little, Daddy'd put a pillow over the crossbar so it wouldn't hurt me to straddle it, and I rode around with him. The bike-a-thon bike was my first real bike, and in the picture, you could tell how proud I was. I was still little, and my skin was still good. Wendy was wearing a helmet, but Daddy and Aunt Glo didn't know I needed one, and I was glad my head was free. That was back before I cut my hair short, so my hair was flying behind me, proud as a flag—a pirate flag, I reckon, or maybe a prisoner of war, since my hair's blacker than Daphne's.

I always liked that picture, but it doesn't look like me. Aunt Glo sent it off to Daddy a long while back, and I wonder if he's got it stuck to his locker. Maybe he traded it for drugs, and now strangers look at me and Wendy and jerk off I'm glad I don't look like that anymore, but I feel a little bit guilty about sending Wendy off to prison without her even knowing.

That was the only day Daddy and Aunt Glo met Wendy. Daddy said she had the personality of a fish, meaning there wasn't much about her to like. But today I think it'd be pretty good to have the personality of a fish, as long as you weren't stupid enough to expect a free meal, and I wish I could dive down where it's dark and cold and where there are so many shadows and hiding places, furry grasses and rocks and shipwrecks.

Most days at Morning Devotionals I sit in the back and don't say a word, just listen to the reading and sing some songs and hold sweaty hands with whoever sits next to me when we do the Lord's Prayer. But today all they want to talk about is the dead girl. They call her by name—Clara Tinsley—and I didn't even know her name because I didn't read yesterday's paper or watch the news. They're still asking questions when the first bell rings, and we have to say our prayer fast.

"We should remember Clara Tinsley's family," Wendy says, so somber, like she knows Clara's momma and daddy personally.

"And Rhonda," I add.

"Who's Rhonda?" somebody asks, and the question vibrates all wrong in my teeth. My head goes swimming and my guts feel so sick, because sometimes it seems like you have to die to make any kind of a difference.

THE LAST FRIDAY OF THE MONTH, we always have assembly. Today it's the prisoners again, telling their stories, trying to talk us out of the criminal lifestyle. They bring the prisoners every year to testify, but I hate it, because they talk about how awful prison life can be, and I can't stand to think of my daddy suffering it. I wonder why my daddy can't go on a bus tour to high schools and tell his story. Then he wouldn't have to deal with gangs or roaches or being treated like an animal.

At the same time, I wouldn't really want him at *my* school.

Aunt Glo says you can't trust those high-school-assembly criminals because they're the worst kind: pure con men, stringing lies and turning on the tears for effect. At least my daddy is sincere, she says, even if he's a weak man.

That's what everybody says—that Daddy's weak. My Granny Eloise down in South Carolina, who can't raise me because her blood pressure's too high, wrote a letter to the judge before his sentencing. Daddy's lawyer got a copy of it, too. "He's a spineless coward," she wrote. "I'd ruther see him in a pine box than in the shape he's in. I hope you lock him up a long time." But Daddy didn't get mad at her, and he told me not to be mad, either. "She's just disappointed," he said. "She raised me right. Weren't nothing wrong with how she raised me."

Aunt Glo popped him against the shoulder. "Stand up to her, Greg," she said. "You don't have to be spineless about *every*-thing!"

But after he was gone, Aunt Glo took me aside and told me how Daddy couldn't help it, he had an addiction, and it made him do things he shouldn't.

It seemed to me just the opposite—like he didn't do things he *should*. Like get up in the morning and go fix somebody's car.

All my life he'd fixed cars, until the year I was twelve and he just quit. He kept saying, "I've got a job lined up for tomorrow," but then the next day he was still sleeping when we got on the bus, still sleeping when we got off it. He drove around all night long playing loud music, and after he lost his license and sold his truck, he rode all night on his bicycle. He hocked all his tools. He and Aunt Glo fought all the time back then, because he sold a special ring she had, a sapphire ring she loved.

Then one day he told us he had a job lined up in New Jersey, helping a fellow move some furniture, and he promised to take us all to the steak house when he was done. He told Aunt Glo that as soon as this job was over, he'd buy her blue ring back.

But none of that happened. There was a sting operation on the interstate, and Daddy and his furniture friend were pulled over with a truckload of bedroom suites. There were drugs stashed in some of the dresser drawers, enough crack cocaine to send him to prison for a long time, fifteen years and eight months when they added in the charge for possessing paraphernalia, even though it was his first offense.

"Maybe he didn't know about the drugs," I said that night at supper, and Tim-Tim snorted and muttered, "You wish."

Aunt Glo said the only reason in the world Daddy was involved in such a thing was his addiction. He just needed a fix.

And if I've learned one thing, it's that we all need our fixes. Some of them are drugs and some of them are other things— tire stems if you're Quincy, sex if you're Tim-Tim.

The principal tries to call us to order, but the microphone's half-busted and needs adjusting again. So it's another five minutes before the guys onstage in their prison jumpsuits get started. They sit in a semicircle in folding chairs, and they go up to the microphone one at a time to tell their stories. The second one looks almost as young as Tim-Tim. They like for us to see the young ones who've ruined their lives.

This boy keeps talking about the "age of accountability." He was only sixteen when he broke into an old woman's house, the same age as most of us, except I'm seventeen because I missed a lot of school when I was nine and got held back. This boy claims it was his friend's idea. They were high. He can't even remember what they'd taken. They beat her and raped her—now he can't believe he did it—but they tried him as an adult. He'll be thirty-seven years old before he's eligible for parole.

At least he's alive. If he'd broken into Jarvis Stanley's house, he might be dead.

I wonder what Jarvis Stanley's fix would be. High-definition TV?

If Jarvis Stanley had been a woman, and Clara and Rhonda had been men, and if they'd come through the window just exactly the same way, it would have seemed different that he shot them.

If Jarvis Stanley's house hadn't been burglarized the year before, he might not have been so quick at the trigger in the first place.

And really, it's all Tim-Tim's fault, because he's the one who broke into Jarvis's house last year. I know that. Quincy knows it, too. Tim-Tim sold his television to some punks down at the old carnival grounds and used the money to take his girlfriend to the AC/DC concert.

But Tim-Tim knows we won't tell. Quincy's his brother, but I'm indebted in a different way. If Tim-Tim gets in trouble, then Social Services will check up on Aunt Glo, and they'll take me away then, and probably Daphne, too. They'll put us both in foster care, and not together, so Tim-Tim knows I'll keep his secrets, any secrets at all.

'Cause my fix is living at Aunt Glo's.

I SKIP LUNCH MOST DAYS because it's hard to get a seat in the cafeteria. People put their jackets on all the empty chairs, and sometimes when I hurry and get a table to myself, a group of boys will run me off.

I don't let it get to me, though. They're like the seagulls that fly from piling to piling, chasing off littler birds. I used to sit with a boy with cerebral palsy, but he transferred. So now I go to Ms. Brady's room—she's been my English teacher for the past two years—and she lets me hang out in the workroom with the yearbook staff.

I'm not technically on the yearbook. I would be if I could stay after school. I'd sell the ads or lay out the pictures on the computer, if Ms. Brady wanted me to. But I go to Tech Center in the afternoons and take the bus home from there, so I can't stay for meetings.

Sometimes Ms. Brady gives me work to do, organizing pictures or proofreading. She'll list me as a volunteer in the acknowledgments page. She tells me this like it matters. "You can list it on your resume," she says.

Every day I bring an apple and a banana in my backpack. I eat my banana first, because it dries out my mouth, and I eat the apple second and chew it a long time. The juice is so good, and I'm so thirsty that I suck on the pulp before I swallow. I've heard that apple seeds contain tiny bits of cyanide, but I suck on them anyway. I keep them under my tongue all through fourth period, and sometimes, if I'm thirsty enough, I chew them up so the bitter will make my mouth water, and I swallow them, too.

IN THE AFTERNOONS, AT TECH CENTER, I take two classes, automotive repair and computers. All we've done so far in automotive repair is change the oil in the teachers' cars. My teacher pretends like I'm not there. He lets the boys change the oil over and over while the three other girls (who signed up for the class so they could be near their boyfriends) lean against the far wall and make jokes. I stand as close to the hood as I can get, peeking around the boys, because one day I might need to get a job at the Jiffy Lube. There's one not five miles from Aunt Glo's, and I could take the transit bus.

All we ever do in computer class is keyboarding and timed writings, where we have to type a certain number of words per minute to pass. The teacher puts up the passage on a big screen in the front and says, "Hands ready"—my nails are bitten to the quick, but not stained around the rims with motor oil like I want them to be—"Begin," she says, and I type whatever statement she copied off of Wikipedia that day: "The lemur is the evolutionary predecessor to monkeys and apes," and on and on. My fingers are long, like my momma's fingers were. When I move my fingers over the computer keys, I watch the tendons in my hands and think about my momma, how she played the guitar and how her tendons stood out when she pressed down the strings.

We sang "She'll Be Coming 'Round the Mountain" over and over. I remember my momma's hands better than her face. I type harder than I need to, and pretty soon I'm typing the lyrics instead of the lemur passage: "Oh, we'll all go out to meet her when she comes." I'm thinking of the calluses on my momma's fingertips from pressing strings with letters, three fingers to make an A, a G. It seemed like an F took her whole hand, one hand working hard, one hand strumming easy. I remember her hands as I return to the passage: "The term 'lemur' is derived from the Latin word *lemures*, meaning 'spirits of the night.'"

When the teacher calls, "Time," in spite of my paragraph, I don't know a thing about lemurs. But all afternoon I'm singing Momma's song in my head.

T HERE'S A CHEERLEADER ON MY BUS, Sudie Montgomery, and on Fridays when we have football games, she wears her little cheerleading costume to school. It doesn't look like anybody ever bothers her on the bus, grabs between her legs when she walks down the aisle or anything like that, and maybe if they did, she could stand up for herself hit them on the head with her pom-poms or something.

But she wears panty hose beneath her cheering costume,

even though it's still September and warm. Maybe she does it to make her legs look tan, or maybe it's another layer of protection.

Her stop is before mine, and since she's on the seat behind me, I can hear her panty hose rub-rub, the softest swishing ever as her legs step out into the aisle, and I can hear her thighs telling each other secrets as she moves off the bus and away. I watch her as she crosses to the sidewalk and turns around and waves to her friend, and I study her legs in those panty hose, naked or nude or suntan, sheer-to-the-waist or control-top, definitely A, not B or queen. I wonder if she's got on panties beneath those hose, or if she wears the kind with panties built inside them. I wonder what she looks like when she takes off that cheerleading skirt and if her boyfriend puts his hands on her there, with nothing but those panty hose to keep his hand separate from her insides. I imagine all her little hairs smushed down dark and flat beneath those hose, and it makes me sad, the way a dead baby bird makes me sad.

When we get to my stop, the first thing I see is that the dead girl's car is gone, and there's an empty place right in front of our house, a big old gap. I'm so thirsty, and my mouth tastes sharp as armpit, but I don't hurry inside to drink, like usual. I go to where her car was parked and I stand right where the front seat used to be. Seems like I can picture riding around in that red Pontiac, and in my mind, it smells like vanilla pudding in there, probably from lip gloss. I can almost hear the radio. In my mind, I open the hood and check the oil, and since it's low, I add a quart. In my mind, I'm working at the Jiffy Lube, and Rhonda and the dead girl bring the car by for servicing. They're both wearing panty hose, and they look at bride magazines while I change their fluids.

Then somebody blows the horn and I'm back on Osprey Lane.

"You holding that spot for somebody?" this man hollers out through his rolled-down passenger window. I think he's Miss Mattie's nephew. I've seen him before.

"No," I say. "Sorry," and I head on in the house, and he parks his banged-up, rewed-up Monte Carlo right in the spot where that dead girl's car belongs.

HERE'S THE THING: There are holes that never go away, holes that never fill back up no matter what. Forever as long as I live, that dead girl's car will be gone. Aunt Glo will park her Ford Escort there. Tim-Tim will save up and get a truck, and he'll park in that same space. One day I'll get a car myself, and when I drive back home to Aunt Glo's house from wherever I'm living, when I come back for Easter or something, I'll be glad to get that spot closest to the door.

But there will still be a hole. I'll be parking in a hole. I'll be parking right on top of where that dead girl's car should be, and even with my car there, a car I can't even picture yet, there will always be an empty place.

I UNLOCK THE DOOR WITH MY SILVER KEY and run straight up to the bathroom. I sit on the pot and drink and drink from my blue cup. It's not a big bathroom, and I can refill my cup without even standing. This is the best part of my day, when I'm home, when I've made it. I close my eyes and sit there awhile, savoring the quiet. Aunt Glo's working at the store, probably till five, and Quincy's already come and gone. He goes to the middle school, where they get out forty-five minutes early so they can reuse the buses. He's probably at the post office with his friends, and if he has to use the bathroom, he'll just pee in the rhododendrons. Daphne stays late for tutoring and rides the resource bus home. She won't be back until four-thirty, so the house is all mine.

I can smell myself, so I take a shower, but I leave the bandages on as long as I can. In the shower, I pretend like they're my skin, and I run the bar of soap right over them, scrubbing harder at the parts beneath my arms, because no matter how much deodorant I wear, they still go sour after a while.

I don't look down when I wash my lower parts, but I let my hands feel the bones that push out of my hips. Back when I was little and stupid, I thought my hip bones were tumors, and I was scared I'd die like my momma died.

I wash between my legs so I won't smell like a girl, but I try to hurry and not touch myself long, so I won't feel like a girl, either.

At the very end of the shower, I take off the bandages and let them drop into the water at my feet. The drain's real slow, so it's kind of like being in a washing machine. I kick them around with my toes while I soap up my chest, keeping my face turned up to the spray so I won't have to see them.

My bandages are all stretched out and don't work as good as they used to. When I'm done with my shower, I roll them up in a towel to get them as dry as I can, and when no water's left dripping, I hang them out the window. I have to hide them from Quincy and Tim-Tim or they'll make fun, so I drape them off the arm that holds the satellite dish against the house. It's right outside the bathroom window, easy to reach, and nobody looks up at a satellite dish. It's like your eyes are trained not to see it.

Back in the room I share with Daphne, I put on my spare bandage. It's made for ankles or elbows instead of knees, and isn't nearly as good as my other one. When I use my spare, I have to reinforce the job with Aunt Glo's panty hose.

It feels bad to steal from Aunt Glo, but I've done it more than once. Control-top panty hose, size B. I've got two pairs hidden inside some rolled-up socks. I cut off the legs, slice a neck hole in the crotch, and wear it like the tightest bra ever. And when Aunt Glo slams around the mudroom, looking behind the dryer, saying, "Have you seen my nylons?" nobody knows I'm suffocating beneath them. I can't hardly breathe, bound up as I am in nude or naked or suntan, some color that almost blends right in.

IT SEEMS LIKE THERE OUGHT TO BE A FUNERAL. That's what I tell Aunt Glo when we're all in the kitchen. She's brought home a newspaper from the store, and the story's right there on the front, along with a picture of Clara Tinsley, who died, and a picture of the company where the rental lady works. No picture of Rhonda, though.

"Don't you think somebody ought to have her a funeral?" I ask.

"They'll give her one back in Georgia, I suspect," Aunt Glo says. "Or wherever her family's at." She's looking at something under her microscope—a fingernail sliver, since she and Daphne have been doing their nails. Aunt Glo's nails are finished, but Daphne's still hard at work. "Check this out," Aunt Glo says, and I squinch my eyes to see the slide she's made. It has a piece of a fake nail and a piece of a real nail. Aunt Glo loves biology and even went away to college to become a biologist. But she got pregnant in her first semester and had to drop out.

"You can't really tell the difference," I say, meaning between the two nails. I'm not even sure which one is which. "Don't you think we should have her a funeral *here?*"

"In the kitchen?" Daphne says. She's taking her turn at the

microscope, adjusting the focusing knobs. *"Shoot,* no. This ain't no place for a funeral." She says it like she's an old lady, like she's slap worn out. Then she gives up on the slide and goes back to pressing on fake nails. They're all too big for her little fingers and make her hands look like claws.

"Seems like we ought to honor her or something," I say. And I'm thinking of a twenty-one-gun salute or even a roadside monument. Sometimes people put up little crosses and flowers at the places where wrecks happen. "Maybe we ought to put a wreath on Jarvis Stanley's door," I suggest.

Aunt Glo cuts her eyes at me and says, "Don't be morose."

It's not a word I've ever heard her use, and I don't want to be morose, so I shut up. She turns off the microscope light, puts the plastic cover back on it so nobody will ruin it with jelly or juice, and slides it toward the middle of the table, where it sits next to the fruit bowl.

Then she says, "Poor old Jarvis." I hate it so much when she defends him like that. "He come to the store today and couldn't hardly eat. Ordered a cheeseburger and onion rings but didn't get down more than a couple of bites." She shakes her head. "I invited him to come with us to the Armory. We'll see."

"No, you didn't!" I say.

"The man's all tore up, Kenny Try to put yourself in his position."

"He killed a girl," I say.

"The police didn't treat him right, neither," Aunt Glo says. "Kicked him out of his own house while they did the investigating. And that gun they confiscated belonged to his daddy."

All of a sudden I'm about to cry, and all my words go crippled in my throat. So I hurry to the sink and start washing dishes.

There's a dance at the Armory on some Friday nights. Everybody goes. But I'm not going, not with Jarvis Stanley. It's bad enough we have to live right next to where it happened. I wish I could explain how it feels, to know that somebody dropped dead right in your air, in the same air you're breathing. It seems all wrong to live next door to Jarvis Stanley and to have to hear him answer the telephone the way he does— "Yellow?"—to hear him belch through the walls as if nothing's changed. I hate him.

"I ain't going," I say. "Not if he goes."

"Suit yourself," Aunt Glo replies.

Quincy comes in and shoves a cookie in his mouth.

"Come 'ere," Aunt Glo calls, and he smirks but goes over and lets her smooch on his head. "You stink," she says. "Get you a bath tonight."

"Yes, ma'am," he tells her, but he won't do it. He won't do it, and she won't know, and I'm mad at them both for no good reason. They can pretend like everything's ordinary, but it's *not*. The faucet leaks water from where it's not supposed to, and even *that* makes me mad. My eyes start running, and my nose. I sop it up fast with the dishrag and try not to choke on things I know better than to say.

"Check this out," Aunt Glo says to Quin. She uncovers her microscope again and lets him look at the real nail and the fake nail.

Quincy laughs a little and says, "Wow"—like he cares.

"Ain't that something?" Aunt Glo marvels, and she looks at her slide some more. Even though I'm aggravated with her, I'm glad she has her little pleasures, her microscope and her fake fingernails to wear when she goes out dancing. She's not allowed to wear them to work anymore since she lost one in the pancake batter and a customer found it all syrupy in his mouth.

While Aunt Glo helps Daphne paint the nails on her right hand, Quincy comes over to the cabinet where I'm putting the juice glasses away and whispers, "Look." He's got four tire-stem caps in his palm.

"Whose are they?" I ask.

"Dead girl's," he says, and I pop him right in the shoulder, hard. He drops the black caps onto the linoleum.

"Hey!" he says, and he hits me back. Then he gets down on his hands and knees to find the one that rolled off.

"You shouldn'ta stole from her," I hiss.

"She don't need 'em no more." He laughs, and this time I slap him with the dish towel.

"Bitch," he says. "You made me lose one."

"Yall quit that," Aunt Glo says without looking up. She's not really listening, either, or else she'd hear us, 'cause we're not that quiet. But she doesn't want to hear. She tunes out a lot.

I get down to help him look for the lost cap. The floor's all gunked up at the edges, dust and hair and pieces of onion skin, a single dried-up pea. "When'd you get 'em?" I ask.

"Right before the man come," he says.

"What man?"

Quincy shrugs. "Man in a wrecker come got the car. Right after I got off the bus." Then he gives up, like that tire-stem cap doesn't even matter. He stands, slips the other three caps in his pocket, and wipes his hands on his jeans. "Save it for me if you find it," he says.

I wonder if it was Clara Tinsley's daddy who came and got the car. But that doesn't make sense. He'd be busy with the funeral down in Georgia. So maybe it was Rhonda's boyfriend or just a man from the service station. Or maybe somebody stole it. "What'd he look like?" I holler after Quincy.

But Quincy's already gone.

Somewhere outside there are clues: dropped hairs, fingerprints, pieces of lint from clothes and dirt from shoes. If I had a microscope strong enough, I could find the man who took Clara Tinsley's car away. But what difference would it make? She'd still be dead.

Later on, I find the tire-stem cap rolled off to the side of the oven. I can't reach it with my fingers, but I manage to dig it out with the handle of the broom.

AT FIRST DAPHNE WANTS TO GO to the dance at the Armory, but then she decides to stay home with me and eat macaroni and cheese straight out of the pot. "Jarvis Stanley looks like an old platterpus," she says.

"Platypus," I say.

"Platterpus," she repeats, or tries to. She thinks she's saying it right. I feel sorry for her and worry that it's my fault she's challenged in the brain department.

When I first moved to Aunt Glo's with my daddy, I thought I had cancer like my momma, and mine was already spreading. It wasn't just my hip bones that had me worried. My titties had swollen up (it seemed like I was too young for them to be growing), and then the nipples dipped back inside my body. I thought for sure it was cancer. Maybe I wanted to die.

There was nobody to tell. I couldn't tell Daddy. He'd be so sad to lose me, after he lost Momma. They cut off her whole chest, and she died anyhow, back when I was littler than Daphne. I'd seen Daddy cry at night for years, leaning on his girlfriends on my momma's paisley couch. I didn't want my daddy to love them. But at the same time, I wanted him to have somebody to love after I was dead.

Me and Daphne clank our spoons against the metal, scraping up the extra cheese. Daphne's mouth is dappled orange, but I don't wipe it. I don't interrupt her as she entertains herself with some Silly Putty, trying to get Clara Tinsley's face off the newspaper, then stretching it wide. I love Daphne to pieces and don't want her to be retarded on my account.

She was still a baby when I moved into her bedroom. There was a crib in one corner and a bed with squeaky springs in the other. That was where Aunt Glo's daughter, Constance, slept, but she was gone by the time we got here. I've only seen her twice in all my life, and both times she had hickeys.

Daphne wasn't quite one, and I wasn't quite eleven. At nights, when everybody was sleeping, I used to take Daphne out of her crib and give her my titties. They were barely growing, swollen lumps that ached so bad. She didn't really wake up. She sucked until she pulled my nipples out. She sucked in her sleep.

I hated the way it felt, but liked it, too, the grabbing. I'd only let her suck a little while, but I did it a lot that first year or two.

I didn't stop until the night I almost got caught.

Aunt Glo came in, and I had Daphne in bed with me. But it was dark, and I popped her mouth off and slid my T-shirt down as soon as the door squeaked open. We were under the sheet together. I told Aunt Glo she'd been crying.

DAPHNE HAD LITTLE BABY TEETH by then and didn't know not to bite. It hurt sometimes, but I thought it'd be good to let it hurt and just get used to it.

She had the littlest teeth, like nubby fish teeth, like that time we caught a blow-up fish out on the pier. Sometimes I get the memory of that fish stuck in my head and I can't stop remembering it, so pale and white and clammy, from the underside of the bay. We had to use pliers to get the hook out.

That fish looked like a drowned baby.

Sometimes I worry it's my fault that Daphne's slow to learn. She still grabs at my chest sometimes and giggles, even though I've got my tits all bandaged away.

DAPHNE WANTS TO WATCH A MOVIE, but I can't stay in the house. It seems like I can smell it, that dead girl's blood. I sniff the cushions on the couch where Rhonda sat, and I get a whiff of something deep inside them that makes me ache so bad in the middle. I can't stop thinking about Rhonda, wondering what she's doing, wondering if she'll go to Clara Tinsley's funeral. I can't stay home.

But I can't go to the Armory, either, not with Jarvis Stanley there. "Let's walk to the beach," I suggest.

Daphne makes a face. "Let's go to the ball game," she says. She means the football game at the high school. That's where Tim-Tim will be, not watching the plays, but out in the parking lot, sitting in somebody's truck with tinted windows and smoking a doobie.

I'm scared to go to the football game, but I don't tell Daphne that. At least at school, there are teachers who sometimes protect you. At extracurricular events, you're just a target for whatever meanness comes your way.

"We don't have a ride," I try, but Daphne reminds me that the Baptist church has a van that leaves at seven.

"We're not Baptists," I say.

"I am," Daphne claims. "I went there for Bible school."

Even if football games were safe, I wouldn't go. It's weird how boys look so mad even when they're happy. They get touchdowns, and instead of smiling about them, they hit each other and grunt and make faces like war.

So I distract Daphne by telling her we need to build a shrine to the dead girl. "A monument," I say, and she loves that idea. She likes crafts and runs off to get her construction paper and glue.

"No," I say. "We gotta collect things from the natural world. Feathers and shells and stuff. Like the Native Americans did." I'm just making things up to get my own way, but I know Daphne studied Native Americans in school. It works. She's all into collecting. I get her a jacket because I can see from the trees out front that it'll be windy down there.

And sure enough, it is, but she follows me anyway.

We walk up and down the beach past sunset and into the

twilight. Daphne talks a mile a minute, telling me about playing kickball, boys against the girls, but I don't listen much. I've learned from Aunt Glo that listening's optional. Daphne finds bits of broken glass, coiled-up coins of seaweed. I hold the grocery bag and she goes off scavenging. When she comes back, I open the bag, and she's still talking about kickball, so she doesn't even look up at me, and that's good.

When we walk into the wind, the wind blows all my tears out. When we turn around and walk the other way, my face dries right off.

Wet and dry, wet and dry, one right after the other. What would I do without the wind? Daphne never notices any of it, and I'm glad. If she saw me cry, she might cry, too, and that'd make everything worse.

WHEN SHE GETS TIRED OF COLLECTING, I take her home and run her a bath. "What about the shrine?" she whines, and I tell her we'll put it up on the one-month anniversary of the dead girl's murder. I don't plan to say that. It's just what leaves my mouth, for some reason, and that satisfies Daphne for the moment.

Daphne's got these crayons that you use to write on the shower walls. They wash right off She draws some pictures on the wall, a cat underneath a flower umbrella, a house with trees like lollipops. The cat's bigger than the trees. She writes her name in yellow, and then she writes it again in green so it'll show up.

I watch her in the mirror and pick at a pimple on my chin that won't come up and won't go down. It's been there three weeks, at least. I can't stand to look at my face all at one time. I can only just look at one little part.

There's so much mildew around the edges of the bathtub that it looks like a coloring-book page, all outlined in black. I remember coloring and trying so hard to stay in the lines, taking my black crayon and pushing down hard on the black lines that were already there, just so I'd know where the limits were.

Looking in the mirror at Daphne behind me, I picture her inside a coloring book, and for some reason, it makes me so sad. 'Cause what if none of this is real? Not me, not Daphne, not Rhonda or Clara Tinsley? What if we're just outlines? And there's nothing in the whole universe but coloring-book pages and mildew?

So I turn around quick. "You ready to get out?" I ask Daphne.

"No," she says.

"Well, hurry up," I tell her. I get her a towel. It's clean but stained up with something dingy, grease from Quincy's skateboard wheels or Aunt Glo's tipped-over blueberry wine. Everything around here's so raggedy, even me. "It's bedtime," I say.

"It is not," Daphne says and keeps coloring.

I imagine taking one of her bathtub crayons and covering up the black mildew growing in the caulk. I picture it blue, and red, and orange, any color but black.

"You have a white crayon?" I ask her.

"No," she says. "Just these," and she holds them in her fist and draws a big rainbow. It arches over the cat with the umbrella and the house and the trees. "You wanna ride down this rainbow with me?" she asks.

"Sure," I say.

So she draws a stick person right at the top of her rainbow, sitting astraddle, and then she draws a bigger stick person behind the first one. "That's you," she says. "And that's me." She gives herself some long hair and loops me some short hair for good measure. "You ready?" she asks.

I nod.

"Whoooosh," she says, and she rushes her arms down the rainbow. "There we go." She giggles. "Hold on." She splashes us into the water.

I wipe my face in the stained-up towel. "That was fun," I say.

"Let's do it again." She erases us, redraws us, and we slide down the rainbow two or three times, face-first, backward, doing handstands. Then we tap-dance back up. She draws us hula hoops and we stand atop the rainbow and hula together in the clouds.

I'VE GOT HOMEWORK, PLENTY OF IT, so I plop down on the couch and read this book for school, a play, really, Shakespeare. It's hard to get into. It's late, but Aunt Glo's not back from the Armory, and Tim-Tim's not back from the ball game. Quincy's got a ten o'clock curfew, but since Aunt Glo's not home, he brings all his friends over to skateboard on the sidewalk in front of our house. When he sees Aunt Glo, he'll hop up on the porch and give her a smile, and she'll forgive him for carousing.

It's still warm out, so the windows are open, and I can hear the hard little wheels clacking on the concrete for a while. But then the boys quit, and they get quiet, then bust out laughing, and one of them says, "That's *exactly* how it feels. I swear it."

"No way," another one says.

In a minute Quincy comes in and hurries through the living room.

"What are y'all doing?" I ask.

He comes back with an orange in his hand. "Nothing," he says.

"You better tell 'em to go home," I say, but he ignores me, lets the door slam behind him, not even thinking of Daphne trying to sleep. He's twelve and a boy. I figure he's hungry. I mean, what else would he be doing with an orange?

When I hear them whispering again, I go sit by the window, where it's easier to eavesdrop, and I look out through the blinds. They don't see me. They're too busy concentrating. Quincy's friend Roger peels the orange, dropping the pieces of skin right on the ground. 'You gotta be real careful," he says. Roger's the same age as Quincy, but he's already hit his growing streak and stands near six feet high. His hand looks twice as big as Quincy's when he offers him the orange. "Try it," he says.

Quincy holds the orange and looks confused. "You just stick your finger in it?"

"Yeah," Roger says. "Hard." Then he snatches the orange back and says, "Like this." He plunges his finger into the place where all the sections of orange come together. He sticks his finger in over and over, and even through the window, it seems like I can hear that orange tear and slurp, and I get the sickest feeling, so I go on up to bed.

SOMETIMES AT NIGHT I PRAY, even though I don't believe in God. There's a streetlight outside the bedroom window, and sometimes when I close my eyes but still see light, without even looking, I pretend it's God. That must be how God works, if God's at work at all, forcing you to believe by defying logic.

You can't see with your eyes shut, but at the same time, you can't help seeing.

Sometimes at night I pray to the streetlight, "Go out."

Sometimes I beg it, "Don't blink."

AUNT GLO AND JARVIS DON'T GET HOME until midnight. I can tell Jarvis is really drunk because Aunt Glo helps him inside. I hear them banging around on the other side of the wall and hope there's not a ghost in there with them.

Jarvis must try to kiss Aunt Glo or put his hands where

they don't belong because she says, "Now, you quit that!" She won't let it get to her, though, like I would. She probably won't even mention it. I don't worry about Aunt Glo and Jarvis Stanley getting together like a couple, because he's at least sixty, and she's only forty-five, and besides that, she loves my daddy, in spite of his weakness. She sends him a crossword puzzle every week.

Water trinkles through Jarvis's pipes. We share the same pipes, so his water's like our water, in a way. That makes it even worse that Clara Tinsley died here, because whoever mopped the floor probably dumped that water out right in his sink. So Clara's blood ran all through our pipes, might still be inside our pipes, and I'm still thinking about her when Aunt Glo unlocks the bolt on our front door and comes upstairs. She brushes her teeth, rinses and spits, drops the lid to her Noxzema in the sink.

I hope that if that dead girl is a ghost in Jarvis Stanley's house, she didn't follow Aunt Glo home. I keep picturing Clara Tinsley dead on that stretcher, and Clara Tinsley in Silly Putty, her cheeks stretched wider and wider until her whole image disappears into a string of putty that snaps in two. I don't believe in ghosts for real, but how can people just disappear? It's gotta take time. Even an old fart hangs around in the couch cushions, and you don't have to make an A in physics to know that just because you can't see something doesn't mean it isn't there. So even though I'm old, I roll up tight like a baby and pull my sheet over my head.

Then I can't get enough air to breathe and have to open a little gap in my covers so fresh air comes through. I wish I could crawl into bed with Aunt Glo, but I'm too old, so I just lay there and worry—because I don't know what I'll do when I turn eighteen.

When I'm eighteen, I won't belong to Aunt Glo. The state won't send her any more money, and I'll be on my own. But I won't even have my high school diploma because I lost a year when I was nine and ten, and I didn't go to school enough to pass because I thought I had tumors and couldn't catch my breath. I was so stupid back then, and now I won't even have a high school diploma to keep me afloat. It's nobody's fault but my own.

So I climb down and get in bed with Daphne. "Move over," I tell her. I'm crying, but she doesn't know it. Nobody ever knows it when I'm crying. What'll I do when I don't have Daphne, when I have no connection to her at all? She's not my sister or my niece either one, not really. It tears me up.

"You old 'fraidy cat," Daphne mutters, from the edges of her sleep. "You been watching scary movies?"

"No," I tell her, and she rolls over next to the wall, and I roll around her and hold on.

In a little while, Jarvis starts coughing. His hacks come right through the walls, ghost hacking. Then he jumps up, and his bedsprings holler, and then he's throwing up.

He keeps at it awhile, big growing *blugh* sounds, with the emphasis on the "ugh," and a long "h" on the end, like he's holding the last note of that vomit a long time. I hate listening to people throw up, but it helps to analyze it, to try to spell it phonetically and get all the emphasis marks in the right places, like Ms. Brady from English class showed us how to do. Sometimes it's like he's saying "bluck" and it turns midway through into "black." Blu-ack. I hold on to Daphne and mouth the sounds and picture them like musical notes.

He staggers back to bed, and I make a decision that wherever I live when I'm eighteen, I'm going to be sure there's insulation in the walls. I wonder how hard it would be to insulate this bedroom, so Daphne won't have to listen to Jarvis vomit for the next ten years.

Daphne kicks and kicks in her sleep, and I worry about her being around so many boys who play with oranges. At least she's littler than Quincy and his friends, so if they look for girls to practice on, they'll pick somebody older, maybe a sixth- or seventh-grader. It makes me worry about Daphne, though, and what she'll do when I'm gone. Who'll watch out for her then?

I wonder about Rhonda and where she is, if she's back in Atlanta with her boyfriend who gave her the ring, and if it feels like he's sticking his finger in an orange when they do it.

Then I get stuck on oranges, picturing that white skin just beneath the tough hide, how fragile it is, and how dry, with the wet meat just below. Seems like if I don't taste an orange, I'll die. I go to the kitchen, my heart racing and my crotch pounding, thinking about Rhonda, but we don't have any oranges left. Quincy used the last one.

So I go sit out on the porch. The wind's picked up. I pull my shirt down over my knees to stay warm, and I watch those little pieces of orange skin blow off the sidewalk and into the grass.

THE VACATION RENTAL LADY lives all the way in Charlottesville, and the house across the street's her second home. She bought it two years ago and spent a long time fixing it up and made all the neighbors mad because she brought in construction crews from out of town and didn't hire our boys to fix the roof She's got long red hair that's the exact same color as her Irish setter, a dog who rides in the front seat of her Mercedes-Benz and sits up as tall as a person. I don't even know she's in town until she comes to the door and knocks and asks if I have time to cut her grass.

I follow her out to the shed behind her place, where she keeps her lawn mower locked up. Even her shed's fancy—they renovated it, too. It doesn't seem fair that some people have two houses and sheds with locks on the doors and other people have to sleep under the pier when they turn eighteen. I wonder if the rental lady would let me live in her shed in exchange for doing handiwork around the place. Maybe she'd move me to Charlottesville and let me be her gardener.

Turns out the lawn mower's out of gas, so I ask if she wants me to go get some. The service station's six blocks away, not very far, but she laughs and says she can drive me.

So I get in her fancy car with her fancy dog and ride to the gas station, where I pump the gas into the red container. She wants me to pump super unleaded, but I tell her that'll ruin her lawn mower and try to explain how motors work. But she doesn't care. She says, "Son, just get whatever we need."

I get a jolt when she calls me "son," a good jolt. People around here know everything about everybody, and all of them know that beneath my clothes I'm a girl. But not the rental lady. If she looked at me good, she might figure it out. I've got long eyelashes that curl on their own naturally, but most times I keep my face down so people don't notice.

She pops the trunk without getting out of the car, and I put the gas container inside next to some shopping bags. As I'm getting in, Tim-Tim rides by and does a double take. I wave in the most ordinary way, but inside, I'm cracking up. What he wouldn't give to ride around in a Mercedes-Benz with leather seats and a compass right up front, digital everything, even a temperature gauge that tells you how hot it is inside and out.

I wait to see if this lady'll mention the tragedy, but she doesn't. She goes on into the house and leaves the dog on the front porch to bark at me every time I pass. I don't care. I love cutting grass. You can see exactly where you've been and where you need to go next. You can't really hurry. You just move steady, one step at a time, and with that lawn mower handle vibrating in your hands, you know you're alive.

If I bought my own lawn mower, maybe people would hire me to cut their grass and prune their trees and bushes, and maybe I could have a landscaping business and support myself that way when I'm eighteen. I could give Aunt Glo some money for rent, and maybe she'd let me stay right there in my bedroom with Daphne. Or if I fixed up the workshop behind Aunt Glo's house, maybe I could live out there with my lawn mower when I turn eighteen.

When I'm done, I walk up onto the porch of 207 Osprey Lane. The dog growls a little but doesn't even get up. He's sprawled out next to the fern, and I remember that the hide-a-key's beneath it. If I ever get really desperate, I can sneak into the rental lady's house and sleep there.

She gives me ten dollars like always and says maybe she won't need to cut the grass again until springtime. So maybe landscaping's not enough to support me unless I start early and save up all spring and summer for the cooler months, when grass doesn't grow.

I slip the money in my pocket and feel something there, the tire-stem cap that Quincy stole. I roll it around in my fingers and linger in her doorway. "That was real sad," I say, "what happened to those girls."

The rental lady makes a face like she's done something stupid, an "oops" face, like she's spilled her drink on a stranger's carpet. "I know," she says. "But you'd think he wouldn't have shot them! He's crazy, isn't he? That man?"

"They were in his *house*," I say, and I can't believe I'm defending Jarvis Stanley, but what else can I do? He's one of us.

"Still," she says. Then she confides, "I guess everybody in this town probably hates me."

I shrug.

"They should've called me, those girls. They had my cell. You can't just go breaking in."

"But Rhonda had the paper right there," I say, "with the wrong address."

"Rhonda?" the rental lady says. Then: "Oh, it was in the other one's name."

Like Rhonda doesn't even matter. In that instant I know that I don't want to be the rental lady's gardener, and I don't want to move to Charlottesville, either. Not ever.

I nod and say, "Well, thanks, ma'am." I move on off her porch, but she calls me back.

"Hey, Kenny?" she says. "If anybody asks, you tell them that I fired my assistant. *She's* the one who put the wrong address on the rental agreement."

I nod again and head on home.

But I can't stay there, not when there's no one to accept the blame. People keep passing the blame back and forth. And I don't even know the name of the assistant who *might have* put down the wrong address. I don't know for sure that she exists.

If she does, I wonder if she's Rhonda's age, right out of school and starting her life, if she has a boyfriend. Or maybe she's Aunt Glo's age, with a family to feed, a boyfriend in jail, and now no job.

Tim-Tim intercepts me in the kitchen, but not for the reasons I expect. He's not envious of my ride in the rental lady's car after all. In fact, he's kind of mad I cut her grass.

"That bitch won't even pay to have Jarvis's house cleaned," he says. "All that blood and brains splattered everywhere. You'd think she'd help him clean it up."

I'm horrified. I thought when the yellow tape came down, after they let Jarvis back in, the place would be clean. "Didn't the police clean it?"

"Ain't the job of the police," Tim-Tim says.

"What about the fire department?"

Tim-Tim shakes his head. "The person left with the *mess* is the one who cleans it up," he says. "But it's her fault." He points across the street. "If she had half a heart, she'd hire a cleaning crew."

"Why doesn't she?" I ask.

He laughs. 'You can't just call the Merry Maids, now, can you? Costs thousands of dollars to have it done professionally, and she claims his homeowner's insurance will pay for it."

I CAN'T STAY THERE, not knowing that a murder took place and nobody even disinfected the spot where Clara's body fell, no bleach, no scrub brushes. For all I know, Jarvis simply shut the door to that room, and there are smidgens of her body still decomposing behind the walls.

It's all too much to think about, and none of it matters anyway. "It doesn't concern you." That's what Aunt Glo would say. But she's asleep on the couch, her cheek slouched over toward the middle of her face, and I can't wake her up.

"Aunt Glo?" I say and prod her. "Aunt Glo?"

She's been sleeping all day. I worry about her, because sometimes she takes those pills that aren't prescribed for her. They're prescribed for somebody else, somebody named Irene Earle, and I don't know where they come from, or if the pills in the bottle match up with what's on the label.

So I get Daphne, and we go fishing, and all afternoon I pretend like Irene Earle is Aunt Glo's secret identity, like she's in the CIA and doing things I can't even imagine when it looks like she's just making barbecue. And maybe my daddy's not really incarcerated. Maybe he just shows up at the prison on the days when we visit, but the rest of the time he's in a Middle Eastern country spying for the government, and we say he's in prison to keep anyone from being suspicious.

I'd like to think there's meaning to all the things that don't make sense.

But more than likely, Daddy's in prison and Aunt Glo's just Aunt Glo. More than likely, Tim-Tim brought her that prescription. Maybe he stole Irene Earle's pocketbook.

Part TWO

THE DOOR WON'T EVEN CLOSE on the workshop behind Aunt
Glo's house. A bungee cord hooks the latch to a nail on the
far side of the wall, and when I loosen it, junk tumbles right
out into the yard—old bicycle parts, doorknobs, an enamel pot.
Inside the doorway, I find a bag of dirty magazines and sections
of an old garden hose cut up to drain the water heater or maybe
siphon gas. It's a mess in there, and when I see how bad it is, I
almost take back my offer to clean it.

"Why do you call it a workshop?" I ask. "Looks more like
a storage unit."

"Used to be where Daddy piddled," Aunt Glo says. "He
made shelves and things back when I was a girl. There's probably
still some tools in there somewhere."

I drag out a broken rocking chair, first the rockers, then the
mildewed wicker seat, and then the spindly wooden back.

Aunt Glo shakes her head. "I don't even remember whose
that was." She sticks her head inside the workshop door. "Ain't
been able to stuff another thing in there for years. Might be
better to burn it to the ground."

I remind her it's a historic structure, and she laughs and
tells me to go for it. So here I am.

I throw a tarp on the grass and start hauling out stuff bit by bit. Every hour or so Aunt Glo comes to see what I've found and says, "Well, I swannee!" or "What in the name of Christjesus is that?" She's lived here her whole life, in the same house, except for a few years when she was married to Constance and Tim-Tim's daddy and stayed with him in military housing.

She finds remnants of fabric that belonged to her momma, but they're so old you can push your finger right through. She keeps an old trowel of her daddy's that he used back when he was a bricklayer, in case Tim-Tim or Quincy decides to give masonry a try. Her momma and daddy were both dead by the time I moved in, but they owned the house first. Aunt Glo officially inherited it when she was thirty-three, and she plans to stay here till she dies, unless they raise the taxes so high she can't, which is something she worries about a lot.

Most things in the workshop are soggy and mildewed. It either flooded in there or somebody left a window open, probably for five or ten years, before they boarded it up.

"Just haul that mess to the Dumpster," she tells me. "Nothing worth saving. Me and Daphne are going up to Wal-Mart. You need anything?"

"Yes, ma'am," I say, and hope she'll figure out what by herself.

But she doesn't. "What?" she asks.

"You know," I say.

"Kotex?" she asks. She says it loud, so loud Jarvis Stanley might hear if he's standing in his kitchen, since the back window's open. I feel that old hot flush, and I nod.

If I had my way, I'd get a different brand, the ones that come in the thinnest sizes and have lots of adhesive on the bottom so they don't slip.

*   *   *

DEEP IN THE WORKSHOP, I find a set of wheels hanging on the wall. They look like old wagon wheels, and they have rusted hinges with the holes already in them. I use a screwdriver to take the legs off a busted card table, and then I attach the wheels to that tabletop. It's rickety and wobbly but sort of like a wagon, and when I hook a rope to the front end, I can pull it okay. So I load things up to drag off to the Dumpster.

The Dumpster's by the corner mart, and it says plain on the side, NO DUMPING. They want to keep it all for themselves, for their stinky old banana boxes, but where else am I supposed to unload this junk? So I sneak back behind the Dumpster and throw my trash in as fast as I can.

By the time the next load's ready, I've talked Quincy and Roger into helping, though I have to promise them each a dirty magazine to do it.

First we hook the rope to Quincy's belt loops. Then I set the kitchen timer to see how long it takes them to get to the corner mart and back. Quincy steps up on his skateboard and kicks off, pulling the wagon behind him. What a racket it makes as he hits bumps, and Roger hollers out, "Toaster in the street—two-point deduction," but he's right behind Quincy to pick it up. Quincy loses a plastic flower pot, a piece or two of wood, but for the most part, we've loaded the wagon right, putting weighty things inside lighter ones to hold them down.

When they come back again and it's Roger's turn, I remind them that speed's only part of the equation. You have to find the right pace that keeps all the objects on the wagon. Roger doesn't fare as well as Quincy because he's so much taller, and when we tie the rope to his belt loops, the wagon's at a steeper angle and more things fall into the street. "Two-point deduction," Quincy calls. "Shovel head in the road!"

This is how I get almost all the junk from Aunt Glo's workshop into the Dumpster without having to spend time there myself.

I don't go to the corner mart unless I absolutely have to. I haven't since I was thirteen. There's a man named Henry who used to stare at me in the big shoplifting mirror and watch me when I walked around the aisles. Then one day when Daphne had a virus and couldn't keep down anything but grits, Aunt Glo sent me there to buy some. "Butter flavor," she said. "Not that artificial cheese and bacon mess!" But they only had variety packs. So I had to ask Henry if he had the butter packs in the back.

He grinned like he always did and said, "Come on. We'll see."

I was a fool to have followed him—because behind those swinging doors, in the back of the store, they just had more boxes of variety grits, not butter.

He said, "I'll give you *all* the butters if you pull your shirt tight and let me look."

"No," I said.

But I was thirteen. My daddy had just gone to prison, and Aunt Glo was keeping me out of the goodness of her heart. It was Saturday, and I'd just woken up, and Aunt Glo'd sent me to the store, and I didn't have on my bra, just the T-shirt I slept in. It was a white one. That was back before I started binding up my titties.

Henry said, "You don't have to pull it up. Just pull it tight."

I didn't know what to do, but I needed those grits. So I pulled my shirt tight, and when I did, my nipples fisted up hard as the heads on nails. I could see them mad and dark beneath my shirt. He looked at me for a long time. He got so close I could smell the sweet rot of his hair. The dirty waves had comb lines and thick flecks of dandruff His mouth was open and hot, breathing cigarettes and sourness on me, his tongue dallying along his bottom lip, so wet, and all that black stubble around his mouth, and his tongue. I couldn't stand it. I would have left, except I was already there.

In a minute, he said, "Butter flavor?" and I said, "Yes, sir," and he laughed. Then he opened all the boxes of variety packs and took out the butters from each box. He handed me so many I couldn't even hold them in my hands and had to carry them in my T-shirt. I pulled it out so far you couldn't tell anymore that I had titties at all.

But the worst thing was he wouldn't let me pay. I tried to give him dollars, but he said, "No charge," and laughed and shook his head. I kept dropping things, packets of grits and dollars, and he just smirked and led me out the back door, not the front.

S OMETIMES I'M GLAD MY MOMMA'S DEAD. At least she's spared the disappointment. It'd make her so sad to see what's happened to Daddy and me, and I couldn't stand that.

Sometimes I think of her fingertips, dented with dark lines from pushing too hard on new guitar strings.

My nipples dipped in, dented, and I thought I was dying like Momma, but I wasn't. (Did I hug her guitar in my sleep? Hold it so tight the strings pressed into my nipples?)

I have her guitar. It's the only thing of hers I have, and I keep it stored away in a black case at the back of the closet. I hardly ever take it out. The year after Daddy went to prison, Aunt Glo got me five guitar lessons for Christmas, but I never went to a single one.

I won't loan her guitar to Tim-Tim, though. He might lose at cards.

I tell Daphne not to play with it. It isn't a toy. But sometimes she sneaks it out anyway and strums all the strings at one time and hollers into the hole, pretending it's a microphone, and I have to let her, since I did her so wrong when she was an innocent baby.

QUINCY AND ROGER HELP ME after school for a while. They even bring some other boys over, and a second wagon, and race against each other. But when all the dirty magazines are gone, they get bored. So by the next week, I'm left carting off the last of the junk myself.

Even Daphne doesn't want to help. She wants to go back to the beach to collect more stuff for the dead girl's shrine. Even though I love the beach, I don't have time to spend there. I don't know how long it'll take to fix up Aunt Glo's workshop, but I want to be done by the time I'm eighteen, in case she lets me live there.

So I give Daphne things out of the workshop for the shrine. She's working on it up in our bedroom, since Jarvis Stanley won't allow it on his porch. I give her a little molded Kewpiedoll head, some old-fashioned railroad bolts, and she arranges them with the shells and feathers she's glued to a pie tin.

Sometimes I imagine how I'll ask Aunt Glo if I can stay. Mostly I think of ways to make myself indispensable. I already do the laundry, collect it from the floors in all the bedrooms, wash and fold it up, and leave it in stacks beside the bedroom doors.

I cook sometimes. I cut the grass.

I tutor Daphne, try to help her with subtraction: If you

have seven crabs and you take away three, how many crabs do you have?

But Daphne wants to practice her math with *live* crabs. So I leave the workshop behind and take her to the beach after all. We catch crabs and put them in the cooler, but when we get them home, they won't stand still for us to do subtraction.

"Shit*fire,*" she hollers. "That little sucker got me good!"

The crabs click all over the sidewalk. They sound like they're wearing high-heeled shoes. They run past the orange peels and hide in the hostas. We have to chase them down and start over. Even Jarvis Stanley laughs.

So we take them in and steam them up instead, pull them out red, and let Daphne practice at the counter. She's okay at subtraction as long as it's not in her head. I don't know how to make her smarter, but I figure if there's any way for me to help her get good grades, then Aunt Glo won't let me go when I'm eighteen.

THERE ARE THINGS IN THE WORKSHOP that I keep—things I can tell have value: an antique sewing machine, steely green with silver plates and shiny bobbins; enormous oyster tongs with worn wooden handles; porcelain dolls; granny eyeglasses; and a set of plates and cups with painted birds. I organize what can be salvaged, wipe off the dust and put the items in clean boxes or plastic containers. There's a tiny bathroom at the back of the workshop, just a broken toilet without any water in it. I stack things on the toilet to keep them off of the floor.

Still other things I keep for Daphne. Like the Styrofoam coolers. They're so old and soft that if you're not careful, they tear. But there are twelve of them. A find. I can't believe it. Two stacks of six up against a wall, and most of them intact; even the punctured ones can be fixed with duct tape.

When I ask Aunt Glo where they came from, she says she doesn't know. "Back when Daddy was on the water, I reckon," she says. "They're probably forty years old."

Forty years, older than my daddy, whose cooler is made out of fiberglass or plastic or something else, something harder and heavy. It's my cooler now.

"Give me a piece of that," Aunt Glo says, and I sliver her a thin strip of Styrofoam. Under the microscope, you can see the individual cells. "It's mostly nothing but air," she says, and she gets quiet after that and puts the microscope away.

I take a kitchen knife and score the Styrofoam along the edges. I cut again, straight as I can, and each cooler gives me two big panels, two littler panels, and a medium-size panel that's the bottom. I cut them up carefully, haul them upstairs, and tack them to the wall behind the bed.

Insulation. For Daphne. For when I'm gone.

I TRY TO KEEP BUSY so there'll be good things in my head, no space or time for the kinds of thoughts that sickos have. But no matter how hard I work, the thoughts come on me, images of dead Clara Tinsley in panty hose, memories of oranges and how they burst when you bite in.

I think about those dirty magazines I gave to Quin. If Aunt Glo finds out, she might not let me stay. But if I'd kept them, I'd have peeked every day at pictures of girls with their legs spread apart.

So I try to keep busy and not think about their fingers touching their hair, those girls made of paper and all of them mildewed, the pages soft as the insides of thighs, and damp like the deeper parts, soft as the pulp of an orange, fine green mold growing on the pages, over their faces and titties, black mildew raised up felty between their legs.

I can't stand it.

I try to stay busy, read Shakespeare for Ms. Brady's class. When it's after dark and I can't see to clean up the workshop, I get some caulk and work on our bathroom, covering up the nasty edges with white cream. But the old mildew stains right through.

I try to stay away from oranges, but sometimes all I can think about is that white fiber that holds an orange together, so fragile, that frosty-looking vein. My heart beats hard to think about it. Fragile as the middle of a butterfly.

I don't want to be a sicko, so I study for the quiz on dramatic structure. When Daddy calls collect from prison, I talk to him about school, tell him about the parts of a play, like I care: exposition, rising action, climax, falling action, denouement. Daddy says, "Well, how about that," and he tells me they have a library at the prison, but he hasn't been to it yet.

I repeat the terms in my sleep—rising action, climax—and I pretend that's how life is shaped, falling action, denouement. If you know the patterns, then everything becomes bearable and everything makes sense.

But it isn't that way at all. Nothing's predictable, not in real life. It probably wasn't even predictable in Shakespeare's day.

Sometimes I get stuck in one place, exposition forever. I can't get to climax to save my life. I get stuck on orange pulp, and orange pulp's all there is. All night long, half the next day, it's nothing but orange pulp for me.

Or I get stuck on Clara Tinsley's blood. I can't help thinking about it. I picture myself crawling around inside Jarvis's pipes, rusty and tinged with Clara Tinsley's blood.

O N FRIDAY IN ECONOMICS CLASS, Mr. Moses gives us an assignment: We have to look in the classified ads and pick out a job we'll be qualified for with only a high school diploma.

Wendy raises her hand and says, "Should we do this even if we're going to college?"

Mr. Moses says, "Yes."

"Can we look for jobs we'll be qualified for *after* college?" Wendy asks, and Mr. Moses says no, we might need jobs to help pay for tuition and books.

Darren Cannon says when he gets out of school, he's going to work with his daddy doing HVAC. "So find an HVAC position and bring in the ad," Mr. Moses says.

"But why do I need an ad?" Darren complains, and Wendy says, "Something could happen to your dad," and then I look down because I'm blushing. She's probably thinking about me.

Sudie Montgomery whispers, "Just get your dad to run an ad," like that's something everybody can afford to do.

I'm already thinking about managing a Laundromat, tutoring children, landscaping, caulking, installing insulation. I'm thinking about Jiffy Lube, where I could change the oil if I could ever get to the front of the class in automotive repair.

AUNT GLO'S IN A REAL BAD MOOD, and she must be aching in her back or in her knees because she stinks like peppermint Bengay. She's got dark bubbles under her eyes, too, probably because she didn't wipe off her makeup from last night. I wonder if it'd be possible for somebody to punch Aunt Glo in the face and us not even know it. She stayed out late again, and I wonder if maybe she thinks about the dead girl all the time, like I do, and if she walks the beach all night just trying to keep from picturing Jarvis Stanley waving around that gun.

Aunt Glo's hair is all matted flat on one side of her head, with a little guinea-pig swirl in the back, and she hasn't even run her fingers through it. She fusses at Daphne for having the cartoons on too loud, and then she hides behind the newspaper. She doesn't even look up when Quincy spills his cereal on the end table. She doesn't notice when he uses her good lace doily to mop it up.

I'm getting ready to go out to the workshop, and when I ask her to save the newspaper for me, she snaps, "Would you give it up, Kenny? You're not gonna find out anything else about that dead girl, so just forget it."

I roll my eyes at Daphne, who's sitting right next to the TV with her ear on the speaker. "I wasn't looking for anything about the dead girl," I reply.

"Yes, you were," Quincy says, his mouth all full of Sugar Smacks. He's poured another bowlful. "You love that dead girl. You're a weirdo, Kenny."

"I am not," I say.

"Leave Kenny alone," Daphne says.

"I am *not* a weirdo," I tell them. "I've got an assignment for school. I need the classified ads."

But Aunt Glo isn't listening. "I talked with Ann Fisher over at the lunch counter about you," she says. "She thinks you need some counseling."

"I do *not* need counseling," I say.

"People notice," Aunt Glo warns, "the way you dress and the way you act. I don't know how long we gonna be able to keep your daddy from finding out. Next time I go see him, you're going, too, missy."

I hate it when she calls me "missy," and I'm *not* going to the prison again. I'm not.

"Look," Quincy whispers and nods to his cereal. "A whole bowlful of little nookies." He dips up a spoonful and swallows it quick. Milk leaks from the edges of his mouth. He thinks he's so funny.

"I want some little nookies," Daphne says. She laughs and jumps up to get a spoon. The Sugar Smacks floating around in their milk do look like little nookies, little fat ones like Daphne's.

Aunt Glo sighs hard, poofing out all her air at once. "There's nothing wrong with counseling," she says. "I reckon it's no surprise, after all you been through, I mean. Ann says we can get you in at the CSB for free."

"I don't need counseling," I say. "I just need the newspaper to do my homework." But she's not listening, and my throat's a clot of madness. I'm not the only one who thinks about the dead girl all the time, and that's not why I need the newspaper anyway, and why won't anybody listen?

Quincy offers me his bowl. "Don't you want some little nookies, Ken? You're a lesbo," and I say, *"I am not,"* and Aunt Glo says, "If Kenny's a lesbian, she's *our* lesbian. Leave her alone."

"I'm *not* a lesbian," I say, but nobody's listening.

Daphne's back with her own bowl of milk, and she dumps the cereal into it. "What do lesbians do?" she asks. My head feels so hot, like all my brain cells are spontaneously combusting, and Quincy says, "I know, I know," real singsongy, and he wiggles his index finger up and down. It seems to me like the world gets so tiny, mildewing around the edges. The world gets darker and darker as it closes in on me speck by speck, and all my brain cells burn to ash.

"I know, I know," Daphne repeats, wiggling her finger, too. She gets right in my face and wiggles her finger, saying, "I know, I know."

She quits when I start crying. "Now look what you've done," Aunt Glo scolds. She rolls up her newspaper and slaps Quincy on the head with it.

Daphne jumps in my lap, but I've got my face turned down. She picks up my face and pats both my cheeks with her hands and says, "Don't be sad, little Kenny." I push her away and run back upstairs and shut myself in the bathroom for a while. I sit against the door and cry onto my knee bones, because I'm not a lesbian. I'm *not*. And why doesn't anybody get it?

W HEN THE PLYWOOD'S PRIED OFF the windows of Aunt Glo's workshop, when the light comes in, I can picture the possibilities of that space. It's not very big, maybe sixteen feet by twenty, but at one time it had carpet, at least part of it had carpet, before the carpet rotted into the concrete slab beneath. And it's plumbed. There's that broken toilet in the far corner and a big grimy sink, the kind you'd use to clean fish. No shower, but plenty of room to take a sponge bath.

The floor's dewy and cold, with a residue of thin mud and some old vinyl squares that I pop up with the end of my crowbar. Sometimes the vinyl squares are rigid and break, and I have to scratch and pry them up in pieces. Sometimes they come up whole. Beneath them, hard scales of glue leave fossils on the concrete.

I dig at the corners of the thin, worn carpet to get an edge up. Then I can tear it back, even roll it up, though the mold beneath chokes me, and every now and again I have to stick my head out the door to catch my breath.

All around the edges there are strips of wood with tiny sharp nails, rusted and mean. The soft wood bends and splinters when I pull it up. I stab myself a hundred times on those nails and drip splats of blood on the damp concrete as I haul it out.

I had a tetanus shot once, so who cares? I'm not stopping for punctures.

The first year we moved to Aunt Glo's, there was a boy at school who carried a pin in his pocket, a straight pin, the kind you use to turn a cuff or mark a line for hemming. At recess, he'd walk past me and stick the pin in my backside. I'd jump, and he'd keep walking, past the gym, out to the field where other boys ran around and threw their balls.

At lunch, he'd stand outside the tray return, and when I came through the chute, he'd be there, hiding behind the trash can. He'd bury his pin in my butt. In and out. So fast it was one motion instead of two. By the time I jumped, cried, "Owee," he was already gone, mingling into the lunch crowd. And I'd be standing there holding my butt and looking like a fool.

On lucky days, when I got on the bus, there'd be a seat in front of him, and I wouldn't have to walk past. He always sat on the aisle, and anytime I had to walk by him, he'd punch that pin in my ass. In and out.

Sometimes I'd holler, "Stop it!" and he'd say, "What?" and the bus driver would shout, "Hey!" and I'd let it go because I didn't want the bus driver to kick me off.

At home, I told Daddy and Aunt Glo, "There's this boy who's bothering me."

"What does he do?" Aunt Glo asked.

"Bothers me," I said.

"He just thinks you're pretty," Daddy said. "That's what boys do when they like pretty girls. Ain't that right, Quincy?"

But Quincy was just in first grade then, so he said, "I don't like girls."

*　　*　　*

SOME OF THE TACK STRIPS BREAK away from the nail that's secured them to the floor, so I have to use the pronged end of the hammer to wedge the nails from the concrete. I pull up nails and wooden tack strips and think of how I'd like to paddle that boy, tie him up and beat him with carpet nails. His name was Clint Willis.

I was brand-new at school and didn't want the girls to know what Clint Willis did to me. It was dirty. They wouldn't want me in their math group or on the library committee if they knew. I didn't want the teachers to know. Girls weren't supposed to let boys stick things in them. Only bad girls did that, girls like Aunt Glo's Constance, and look what happened to her.

The next year he did it in the gym, when we were dressed out for PE. There weren't even pockets in our burgundy gym shorts, so where did he keep that pin? Did he weave it through the elastic in the waistband of his shorts? And if he did, didn't it hurt during sit-ups? He walked past me during volleyball games, poked me with that pin, and I sucked in my air and held it. It was like getting shots every day. But diabetics handled it. I could, too. It was practice for getting chemotherapy. My momma didn't complain. People stuck needles in her all the time, and there was nobody for her to run tattling to.

But I couldn't stand thinking of that pin. Clint Willis licked it. Sometimes on the bus, when I'd turn around, he'd have the pin in his mouth like a toothpick, and he'd see me looking and smile and rub it against his tongue, back and forth. He'd suck on the pin that he planned to bury in my skin the next time he got the chance.

Then one day Clint was gone. We found out later that he went to foster care, somewhere else, in the next county, after his parents lost custody. And I don't even sympathize. I don't care if he has to sleep in a drainpipe when he turns eighteen.

I DIG THE NEWSPAPER out of the trash can and shake off the coffee grounds.

No experience necessary for the pest and termite inspector, but termites make my skin crawl, and I don't want to smell the chemicals or catch cancer from being exposed day in and day out.

The housekeeper must love dogs and have own transportation, eight bucks an hour, criminal background check. But can I say I have a car when I don't? Does the bus count if the bus goes by the house that the housekeeper keeps?

And do I automatically have a criminal background if my father is a convicted felon? It's not the kind of question you can ask out loud in class. What, exactly, is a criminal background?

Then there are entry-level FUN JOBS making five hundred dollars a week, but even I know it's bad news if they don't describe the fun, 'cause fun's not fun to everyone. There's always someone who's the object of the fun, and I don't plan to be that sucker. No way, not me. Beside that, Ms. Brady in English class taught us that using all capital letters is the same as SHOUTING and to avoid it.

I need a quieter job, maybe on the warehouse crew. Must be able to lift seventy-five pounds. I can lift Daphne, but I'm not sure what she weighs. I can lift Quincy, but he's quick and flips me when we wrestle, or when we used to.

Deckhands to three hundred dollars a day—and I saved those antique oyster tongs I found out in the workshop. I could stand on the wooden planks stretched across the boat and tong for oysters. But then my arms would start to look like TimTim's the winter he tonged, and I don't want to grow into Pop-eye. I'd take the muscles, but not the attention, so I scan on down the page.

EXOTIC DANCERS,
NO EXPERIENCE NECESSARY,
MAD $$$.

Vending-machine installation. Banquet servers. Local Herbalife distributors. I finally settle on armored car delivery guard. Nine twenty-five an hour, and I wouldn't have to drive. Just ride along in the passenger seat and have my gun ready in case. They'd give me a gun, and then I'd *have* one, a pistol, probably in a holster. We'd pick up money from banks and deliver it to other banks. We'd pick up diamonds from vaults and transfer them to jewelry stores.

I'd carry a gun, but I wouldn't put any bullets in it. I'd smile at the children and wouldn't look dangerous, except when a gangster came by. Then I'd square my shoulders, hand on my pistol, threatening.

I'd get to wear a uniform. I'd ride around all day listening to the radio. And I'd have a gun, so no one would mess with me.

I THINK ABOUT JARVIS'S GUN A LOT, especially at night, the gun he used to shoot Clara Tinsley, not a pistol but a shotgun with a long steely barrel. The police confiscated it, but Jarvis complained. It wasn't a murder weapon but a weapon of self-defense. How was he to know the intruders weren't armed?

The police didn't give it back, even though it was his daddy's gun, a special one. His gun sits on a shelf somewhere, a tag around the wooden stock identifying the crime and victim, anonymous among all the other tagged guns on all the other shelves.

"It ain't right," Tim-Tim says.

"Shore ain't," Jarvis agrees. They're out on the porch, discussing the obvious: guns, pussy, and NASCAR. That's what men talk about.

"Just goes to show you," Tim-Tim says. "You should never use a gun you love."

"Won't be worth a damn thing when I get it back," Jarvis says. "*If I* get it back."

"Oh, you'll probably get it back in a year or two," Tim-Tim tells him. "But it'll be ruint. Gone to rust."

"You know what I think?" Jarvis says. "If they take your gun, they ought to have to maintain it."

"I can getcha a replacement," Tim-Tim offers.

'You can't replace *that*," Jarvis says. "That thing belonged to my daddy."

"I mean I can getcha another gun," Tim-Tim says. "Everybody ought to have at least two guns, in case one of them's involved in a crime."

*　　*　　*

SOMETIMES I THINK ABOUT how it would be if Jarvis had used his gun the first time, when Tim-Tim broke in, if we'd have seen Tim-Tim on that stretcher pushed dead through the porch light.

I wouldn't have wanted that to happen. I wouldn't want him dead.

When we were little, he used to play dead to scare me. He'd lay so still in the leaves in the backyard, acting like he fell out of the tree. He'd loll his tongue to the side of his mouth and hold his eyes so still, round and brown, he'd let them go glassy, like the eyes in the deer head on the wall. I'd stand over him and holler, "Get up." I'd even pull him by the leg, but he'd keep on pretending until I screamed. Then he'd laugh so hard.

I didn't ever see my momma dead, so that's not why I screamed. I've never seen anybody dead except that one girl Jarvis Stanley shot.

I wouldn't want Tim-Tim dead.

On Aunt Glo's saddest days, when she thinks about Constance and worries her only daughter's a skeleton decomposing somewhere in a field, when she walks around ranting and crying and wondering what she did wrong, there's nobody but Tim-Tim who can cheer her up. Daphne tries, but then she gets upset herself and cries hiccups into the couch cushions. Quincy looks worried and rubs her arm and says, "It's all right, Momma," but in a little bit, he tiptoes out the back. I bring her ginger ale and open the windows to get fresh air inside. I put on the DVD *I Love Lucy*, but it doesn't make her laugh. Only Tim-Tim helps. He puts his muscled arm around Aunt Glo, he walks her around the yard, and when nothing else works, he gives her more of Irene Earle's medicine to tide her over until the bad mood breaks and she acts like herself again.

You can tell how much Tim-Tim loves Aunt Glo by how he lies to her, too, telling her he's saving up for truck-driving school, the kind of lies that will make her proud. Or the way he brings her home the things he wins playing cards, like the fancy white cat he brought home in a crate one time. He doesn't have to do that.

For a while Tim-Tim was like my brother. When I moved in with Aunt Glo, he and I were the same height, even though I was younger. We played Siamese twins and walked around with our heads pushed together at the top and made Daddy and Aunt Glo laugh. We stood with our heads pushed together, standing over the trash can and peeling oranges, dropping bits of orange skin into the trash.

B ACK IN ECONOMICS CLASS, Mr. Moses asks us to report on our jobs. Suddenly I'm not sure armored car delivery guard is right, and what if they all make fun of me? I don't want a gun. What if I shot somebody by accident? *Don't call on me, don't call on me,* I think, and maybe Mr. Moses reads minds, because he doesn't.

"Delivering newspapers," one boy says.

"Do you have a car?" asks Mr. Moses.

"No," says the boy. "But I'll have one when I graduate."

"How will you pay for it?"

The boy shrugs and then says, "I'll just borry my grand-daddy's truck, then, until I make enough money."

"Okay," says Mr. Moses, "but you have to subtract gas and maintenance from your salary."

"Damn," the boy says under his breath.

Wendy will work as an office assistant for a busy medical office, and yes, she has transportation because she recently had a birthday and got a brand-new Camaro. Everybody's been talking about it, even Tim-Tim, who knows her daddy, Dino Honeycutt. Dino Honeycutt is a developer and owns everything that nobody else owns—and some of what they used to. Aunt Glo wants Tim-Tim to "get on" with Dino Honeycutt. If you can do that, you're set, in a good job forever. Back before my daddy went to prison, Aunt Glo wanted him to get on with Dino Honeycutt, too. So it's surprising that Wendy wants to work as an office assistant in a busy medical office, given that she could probably ask her daddy to buy her a medical office, and he'd snap his fingers and there'd it be.

Mr. Moses asks Wendy about the responsibilities, and of course she's called the number on the ad, so she knows exactly what they're looking for. In addition to a friendly disposition, she has to be able to handle multiple phone lines, do some filing and word processing, and be tolerant of other people's differences.

Darren Cannon, who's sitting behind me, pokes me in the back with his pencil and says, "That means you, queerbait."

"It does not," I hiss, but I can hardly breathe. In my mind, I say to Mr. Moses, *Please don't call on me.* I want to be invisible. Not different. I want to be able to sit in a busy medical office and have no one notice me at all.

Sudie will work in day care. Noah will get on with the highway crew. Grady will invest the money his grandmother left him, and he'll open a fast-food chain. For homework, we will calculate our weekly, monthly, and yearly salary and begin looking for apartments. "No more than a third of your income," Mr. Moses says. "That's all you can spend in housing. So configure your salary, give yourself a two-month nest egg, and then look for a place you can afford."

"My daddy's building me a house when I get married," Sudie says.

Mr. Moses rolls his eyes and says, "Do it anyway."

"What if we're going to college?" Wendy asks again.

"Calculate the cost of room and board."

I don't ask Mr. Moses anything. I just hand in my homework—the job ad with a description of responsibilities along with everybody else. Mr. Moses doesn't acknowledge me at all.

W HEN YOU COMING FOR A VISIT?" my daddy asks on the phone, but I don't know. I sit out on the porch swing and tell him, "I don't know," and he says he misses me and wishes his transfer'd come through. There's a prison much closer to where we live, and he's requested it every year at his annual review.

But it hasn't come through. It never comes through. It's all about space and probably money, and we don't have money to spare, not much extra to put into his account so he can buy cigarettes, not much for phone calls, so "I better let you talk to Aunt Glo," I tell him and pass the phone away before he has a chance to say goodbye.

I don't know if I want his transfer to come through.

If I didn't know he was in prison, I could pretend he was at a basketball game. That's what it sounds like behind him, the shouts and calls coming through the phone. I try to picture him at a basketball game, but in my dreams, he turns into the ball itself, round and orange, and other men dribble him against the floor and toss him up through the hoop. They pass him back and forth to one another, slamming him hard.

IN AUNT GLO'S WORKSHOP, there are wooden cabinets all along one wall. Inside I find some tools: a handsaw, screwdrivers, another hammer, a level. I pull these things out so I can clean.

Daphne helps for a while. We find all these Gerber baby-food jars full of nails and screws and nuts, and while I scrub inside the cabinets, Daphne separates the hardware into piles.

"Look at that little old hinge," she says. "Like a rusted-up butterfly." She plays with the hinges, clacking them together and flying them around.

"Move," I tell her. "You're standing in my light."

"Move," she mocks. "You're standing in my light." She clacks her butterfly so close to my ear that it pinches, and I shove her.

"Shut up," I say.

"Shut up."

Inside the cabinets, I find spiders, some living and some dusty dead, their old webs furry and forgotten. I've got a bucket of water with some Spic and Span and some sponges that fleck away as I wipe up spills and stains from some other time, back before I lived here, before Daphne was even born.

Against one cabinet wall, in the very back, there's some kind of strange black cocoon.

"Ugh," Daphne says when I show her. "Nasty."

I'm careful as I wipe at it, but it's stuck there, shellacked. I take a metal file and poke, but nothing's inside.

"You reckon it was a butterfly?" Daphne asks.

But butterflies are soft. "Maybe some kind of beetle," I say, because it reminds me of a beetle, the hard blackness that I know would be shiny if I had better light. It reminds me of the chewing tobacco that drips out the corner of Jarvis Stanley's mouth and dries on his face when he falls asleep on the porch. I wish we didn't share a wall with Jarvis Stanley, because who can say what's growing inside his cabinets? It makes me mad at Aunt Glo's brother, Roy, a man I've never met. He sold his half of the duplex to Jarvis Stanley years and years ago, and now we're stuck with him for good, like he's family, but he's not.

(But then neither am I.)

I always meant to buy it back when I grew up, scrub it top to bottom and make it my own home. But now that Clara

Tinsley has died there, I don't ever want to go inside again, especially knowing that specks of her might still be in there. He ruins everything, Jarvis does. Sometimes he ruins them twice.

I can't stand to think there are creatures living all around us that we don't even recognize or know about. Things we can't imagine, born from black cocoons or dying there, festering and hardening in the walls. Maybe it was a bat that died in the cabinet. I don't know what happens when bats die. I don't know if their wings make shrouds for them to disappear inside of.

Daphne wants to help me, so I give her the metal file and let her chip away at the thing that could be poisonous, for all I know, or could be nothing at all, and she makes disgusted noises, yucks and icks. She laughs and crumples her face and sticks out her tongue. Her tongue's all white because she's got a bad throat, and she's missing four teeth in a row on top, and she looks a little bit like a monster herself. She could have been born from a black cocoon, but I love her all the same.

THERE'S A RUMOR GOING AROUND school that Ms. Brady's changed her name. I've known teachers before who got married and took on their husband's name or else got divorced and took their old name back. But I've never known anybody who changed her first name.

And I'm not sure why it matters, since I never used Ms.

Brady's first name anyway. I always knew her first name—Margie—even before I was in her class, but no way would I use it.

So when someone in Morning Devotional offers her up as a prayer request, saying Ms. Brady's changed her first name to Saraswati, I don't know what that means, or why she would do such a crazy thing.

"Maybe it's a joke," I offer.

"She might be in a cult," Wendy explains. "Sometimes people in cults take on new names."

But Saraswati?

If I were in a cult, I'd pick a better name than *that*.

People make fun of Ms. Brady behind her back. They draw pictures of her wearing a turban, and I feel guilty, but I make fun of her, too, saying "Saraswati" and rolling my eyes. Somebody goes to the library, looks up the name, and finds out it's a Hindu goddess. Somebody else passes around a picture of this woman playing a guitar-looking thing, and someone writes in blue ink below it: SARASWATI BRADY.

Ms. Brady doesn't know, or if she does, she doesn't let on. She smiles in her same old way. She wears her hair in her same old way, and I wonder if I could pretend not to know when people make fun of me. If I pretended long enough, maybe it would come true. I *wouldn't* know. And then I could be happy, the way I was happy when I was little, way back before Momma died.

I wonder if in her secret life, Ms. Brady plays guitar.

She couldn't be a Hindu goddess if she tried, being so blond and blue-eyed. But maybe nobody told her, so she's still free to be like she is in her dreams.

In my dreams, I don't have a body at all, and I don't want one. In my dreams, I'm nothing but energy, a whoosh that rushes around, something people feel but don't see.

Late at night, when everybody's asleep but me (and sometimes Aunt Glo), when I've gotten up to drink at two and can't fall back asleep, I walk down to the pier and whisper to the fish, "Saraswati." It sounds like something a fish might understand.

D APHNE'S BEEN PLANNING THE CEREMONY for a long time, so when the one-month anniversary of Clara Tinsley's death rolls around, I do what I promised. I wake her up early— because it's a school day—and carry her shrine out to the bay because Jarvis Stanley won't let us erect it in his living room or on his porch. (Daphne asked, but he doesn't like the idea of building a shrine to the dead girl. *"Hell* no," he said.)

Daphne's wearing a party dress, a white one even though it's October, and sling-back shoes that look like some Aunt Glo used to have before she lost one on her way home from somewhere. Now the lonely one sits behind the door where she stepped out of it, making friends with dust mites.

I stuff a jacket for Daphne in my backpack, in case she gets cold, but little kids never get cold. They can be standing there shivering and blue-lipped and not feel the cold. I wish I was still little and adaptable. I rub my hands together to keep them from stiffening up.

It's dark out, the moon still hanging around, a good time of day, before everybody wakes up and ruins it. We walk along slow and take a detour through an alley so we can peek at other people's sheds. Some of them have shutters on the windows, and I wonder how much shutters would cost, and whether, if I made nine twenty-five an hour and paid for a security deposit and the first month's rent, I'd have enough to buy shutters and groceries both.

I've got Pop-Tarts in my backpack, and when the sun's up, me and Daphne can eat our breakfast out by the water. Everything seems perfect, and I wonder why we waited a whole month to install the shrine for that dead girl, and I think maybe we should build her a new one every day.

When we get to the beach, Daphne drops right down in the sand and starts pushing sand, making a big castle. Then she arranges her things—shells, nuts and bolts, a pie tin with macaroni glued on, a receiver from a telephone with a long knotted-up cord. "Poor old Clara Tinsley," Daphne says. "Dead." She sticks some feather quills into the holes in the receiver's mouthpiece.

"And Rhonda," I say. I push sand, too, to give Daphne a big raised space for her shrine.

"Rhonda ain't dead," Daphne says.

"Still."

"She don't get no shrine," Daphne says.

"Why not?" I ask. "She survived a terrible thing."

Daphne says, "So did we." Then she thinks a minute and decides I can build Rhonda a shrine, so long as it's not as big as the one for Clara Tinsley. I have to go off by myself to find the shells and things because Daphne's busy. She's got the Kewpie doll's head, and I guess it represents Clara, because Daphne's buried it in sand to the eyebrows.

I don't mind scavenging for Rhonda's shrine alone. I like the walk. There's nobody else around, and I can wander a long way and still look out for Daphne. I spot some dolphins out in the channel, but then they swim on by.

I pick up a crab claw, then another one. I don't think about it. An oyster shell, a broken whelk. Ahead of me, hovering over the water, there's a water woodpecker, not going anywhere at all, steady as a hummingbird looking for fish, white tufts slicked back. Then he dives. I don't know where he goes after that.

I know his real name—kingfisher—but "water woodpecker" seems like a better fit.

When I get back, Daphne's already made me a sand castle mound to plant my crab claws into. I stick them in all directions. "For Rhonda," I say. I've picked up the tail of a horseshoe crab, separated from the body. Most people think of a crab tail as a flimsy thing, but horseshoe crab tails are different. This one is a serrated knife, sharp as an ice pick at the tip, rigid, about six inches long. I use the sharp tip to write RHONDA in the sand.

Daphne's rifling through my backpack, digging out breakfast. "Write CLARA," she demands.

So I write CLARA TINSLEY in the sand, then RIP.

"Where's the coffee?" Daphne asks.

"I didn't bring coffee," I say.

She puts both hands on her hips and cocks her head at me like Aunt Glo might do. "Damn you, Kenny," she says. "How am I supposed to swallow my breakfast without any coffee?"

I ROLL UP THE HORSESHOE CRAB TAIL in a bandanna and take it with me to school. It gives me a powerful feeling, just having it there in my backpack, in the zippered pocket on the inside. It's so sharp at the tip, like it's been filed that way, and there are tiny thorns all along the upper ridge. It's the color of a wooden canoe and shaped kind of the same, except one end's a pointy horn; the other end's more like a bone, pulled away from its socket.

I think of it on the bus when Darren Cannon shoots rubber bands at my head from behind. He doesn't know it, but I could stab him between his ribs, jam that sharp tip straight in his heart if I wanted to, and wouldn't he be surprised.

We're not allowed to carry weapons to school, but some people do. One boy I know got suspended for the whole year when he accidentally left his rifle in his truck. He was in history when they found it. He'd been duck hunting that morning and forgot to swing by home to drop it off. He was almost innocent.

Me, I'm guilty, but nobody will find my horseshoe crab tail, and if they do, I'll say, "It's a rudder." I'll tell them I brought it to school to show the biology teacher.

I take it out at lunch, when I'm in the yearbook workroom and Ms. Brady (Saraswati) has gone to the office to make copies of the Shakespeare test.

I sniff it, but it doesn't smell. The wider end where it connected to the horseshoe crab's body looks kind of like a snout. I sit it on the table and look at it, at the tiny little blond hairs at the very base, and I wonder if they're like the pubic hairs on people, and I wonder if Ms. Brady (Saraswati) will come in and catch me with it.

I wrap it up before she returns and wipe the sand that pours out of the tail onto the floor. The tail is hollow, at least part of the way, and a good bit of sand has gotten inside it. All that afternoon I keep it in my pocket, wrapped in its sheath. I like to feel it there.

In automotive repair, the boys work on a fan belt. The girls unpack boxes of motor oil and take inventory of how many quarts of high-mileage we have. I stand at the station desk observing, and when I move my leg, I can feel the tail hard against me. I stand next to the wash station, fiddling with the greasy container of GOJO, and I think of my daddy. I've heard the rumors about prison life, what happens to men. I've seen the movies. I hope my daddy has a weapon, maybe something homemade, something to keep the other prisoners away.

When I was little, GOJO was my favorite smell. It meant Daddy'd been working, but now he was done. It meant clean hands and suppertime, and it smelled as good to me as Momma's fried chicken. In my mind, all these years later, I still think of those smells together: GOJO and fried chicken. I'd watch Daddy's hands, still glistening from the GOJO, holding that chicken leg up to his mouth, and I'd pull off the thigh skin and eat it in one big crunchy slick gobble.

I sniff the GOJO deep and listen to the teacher fuss at a

boy for not remembering to tighten a screw, and I wonder if a horseshoe crab tail could make it through the mail, if I sent it to Daddy, if I pretended it was part of a science project and maybe put a blue ribbon in the envelope so the prison officials would think I won a prize and wanted to tell my daddy about it. Mostly we send him jokes and word searches, things that fit in envelopes with letters. I haven't written him in a long time and wonder if I could send him just this one horseshoe crab tail, with its snout on one end, its sharp tip on the other. Maybe when he opened it, sand from home would spill onto his shoes. "Wash up," says the teacher, and I pass the GOJO to the boys.

"Thanks, Kenny," one of them says, but most of them ignore me, elbow me out of the way, clear their throats, and wash their dirty hands.

I'M AWAKE IN THE NIGHT, sitting on the porch and looking over at the empty vacation rental property across the street, where Rhonda and Clara should have slept and where nobody has rented since. The outside light stays on all the time, so it's easy to see the withered-up fern that nobody waters. Most of the green parts have fallen off, leaving only the scraggly brown arms.

It makes me think of chemotherapy.

The fern's looking so bad that one day the trashman might

pick it up off the doorstep and throw it in his truck, and then the key to the house would be sitting there exposed. I'm picturing it all in my mind when I hear a noise that turns out to be Aunt Glo.

She's been in bed for a while, so I guess she had a bad dream, or maybe she remembered something in her sleep that she's been trying to forget. I've got our porch light off, of course, so she doesn't see me when she stumbles out the door wearing her housecoat and bedroom shoes. She's got her hand over her mouth to try and hold the sounds inside, but they're coming out anyway.

My heart pricks like it's full of holly, to hear her so upset. When she trips over a tree root, I almost call out, but she catches herself in time, and I don't.

I follow from way behind, in case she's drunk or sleepwalking, in case she decides to lay down in the road and wait for a truck to run her over.

She walks the two blocks to the bay. She goes right through the dunes, over the high sandy hill where you're not supposed to walk, her housecoat belt dragging behind her. I love Aunt Glo and don't want to lose her, but I take the long way around the dunes and along the path because there are horrible sandspurs in those grasses this time of year, brown sharp ones.

Maybe Aunt Glo's beyond physical pain. Or maybe Irene Earle's prescription makes it tolerable. I don't know what it is that makes her so sad, but when she gets this way, I always think of Constance. At least Clara Tinsley's family had a body to bury. Or most of one.

The moon's up high in the sky, but it isn't a bright moon or full, and I can't be sure of anything except her figure in the darkness, how it moves along the shoreline, how her crying sounds otherworldly, inhuman, maybe the way a dying star would sound.

I DON'T WANT AUNT GLO TO GO off the deep end. If she goes off the deep end, we're all in deep shit. Tim-Tim might get custody of Quin, but he'd take him to dogfights and teach him to gamble and buy him women at the carnival grounds. There's no telling what would happen to me and Daphne. They'd put me in a group home, probably, with girls who'd want to fight. They'd put Daphne in foster care, and who knows who she'd share a bedroom with then.

If Aunt Glo goes off the deep end, I'll have no rights to Quin and Daphne at all. It scares me to think they might even find Constance and give Daphne back.

So I call the store where Aunt Glo works and tell them she's got the flu. I bring the microscope to her in bed, on a wooden tray, and I collect things for her to look at: seaweed, algae, froth from the surf I prepare her slides, wet mounts and dry. "Look," I tell her.

I get her a sketch pad and pretend to be a teacher. "Draw what you see," I say, and she looks and looks into the microscope but doesn't move the slide around and doesn't draw a thing. Sometimes I think she's fallen asleep that way. It's like she's balancing her whole body on the bone above her eye. You can't see anything when you look in a microscope like that. Nothing but your own eyelashes.

It terrifies me, how close to the deep end she gets.

The night that Jarvis Stanley blew Clara Tinsley away, I was right there and yet not. I was a part of the story but outside it. I'm that way with Aunt Glo, too. I'm right here adjusting her pointer so she can see the little bubbles moving inside the algae, things too tiny to believe, just living their lives. But I have no idea about the bigger story.

After Jarvis shot Clara, when the police were gone and Rhonda was gone, there were no updates. Nobody called or wrote us letters or filled us in on the bigger story. It happened so close that I smelled it, that hot fear I hope to never smell again. I heard it—not only the gunshot but Rhonda beside me on the couch, her shallow whimpering, gasping, really, like a dying deer. I watched her shiver at the same time sweat curled behind her ear and plastered the little hairs too short for her ponytail to her neck.

I was that close.

But I'm not entitled to a thing beyond that moment. So if Aunt Glo goes off the deep end, I may never see Daphne again, may never know what happens to Quin. Aunt Glo is the only thing connecting me, that thin vein at the center of the orange.

"Look at this," I tell her, and I peel an orange and put the fiber under the microscope. But it's too thick for the light to come through, and I know that, magnified, it's nothing but a blob.

"Huh," she says. She clears her throat and sniffs hard and looks again, like she recognizes what it means.

I KEEP THE HORSESHOE CRAB TAIL for almost a week before I take it back to the beach. It isn't good, how much I think about it, how I hold it in my sleep and run my thumb over the tip. Or how I test its strength, stabbing it into an orange, to make sure it's strong enough to pierce tough skin. It isn't good how I fantasize about being there with Clara Tinsley and Rhonda, somehow in that house. And when Jarvis Stanley waves that gun, I'm there behind him with my weapon, the sharp tip at the side of his throat.

In my fantasy, Jarvis gets so still. He's scared to move. He inhales. He holds himself like a statue, not wanting me to bury it in his throat and break him open. Because then not only will he die, but before that, he'll have to admit how hollow he's always been.

So I take the tail to the beach before it turns me into a psycho killer. I don't really want to be a psycho killer, and plus that, what would happen to Daphne if I went to jail?

The shrine we built for Clara Tinsley is still there, though there are footprints around it, and someone has added a broken green bottle. We built it up close to the dunes, so it'll take a storm or a full moon's high tide to wash it away.

It's not good for me to keep picturing Jarvis Stanley,

stopped still and scared, weapon at his throat. I'm too close to turning sicko when I think about that moment—that private place—the second before you get hurt bad, and you know how much trouble you're in, because you can see what's about to happen, but you don't have the first bit of power to change it.

I can't decide whether to put the horseshoe crab tail in Rhonda's shrine or Clara's. Clara's dead anyway, so maybe Rhonda's the one who needs an honorary weapon. I search the beach in case there's another one, but it's not that common, finding only the tail. It seems disrespectful to break one off the carcass of a whole horseshoe crab, even if it's already pecked clean by the gulls. So I put the one tail right between them, the sharp end erected toward the sky. But then I worry about somebody tripping, maybe Aunt Glo in the middle of the night, stumbling over the shrine and landing heart-first on that sharp tip.

I throw it back in the water. I throw it as hard as I can. But being lightweight and partially hollow, it doesn't go out very far. It might wash right back up in a day or two.

SOME DAYS I THINK ABOUT the dead girl's Pontiac and obsess about where it went. While I'm painting the workshop—ceiling, walls, what's left of the trim—I imagine all the things that might have happened to her car. Did somebody drive it back to Georgia along with her suitcase? Or did her parents sell it—maybe because they couldn't stand to look at it anymore?

I slurp up paint on my roller and mash it out smacky against the walls. It sounds the way Darren Cannon used to sound on the bus when he leaned in behind me to clabber his tongue around his mouth, imitating sex noise to drive me crazy, his fat tongue up close to my ear.

He doesn't do that anymore.

I paint the workshop white, all the same color so it doesn't matter if I mess up. And if the corners are darker where the roller can't reach, who cares?

While I'm wrapping my roller in plastic so it'll be wet and ready for the next time (a trick I learned from Daddy when I helped him paint the kitchen—back before he cracked out), I think about car graveyards. They're all over the place, dead cars sitting there until someone strips them for a bumper or door.

On the school bus, when I'm scratching paint flecks from around my cuticles, I keep an eye out for Clara's car, even though I know it isn't likely her car's gone to scrap. I say a secret prayer that the bus driver will catch pneumonia—not the serious kind but the kind that keeps you in bed for a week—so we'll have a substitute driver. The substitutes always take the long way home, turning on to Bay Ridge Road before coming into town, and that way we pass a place called Mortie's Automotive. Even though the bus hasn't turned that way since she died, I wonder sometimes if Clara's car might be in Mortie's lot, wedged between the ditch and the driveway with the cars they've repaired or the ones they can't.

When I run out of paint and Aunt Glo takes me to the hardware store, I stare out the window hoping we'll pass a car carrier and maybe I'll see that little red Pontiac on it. But car carriers usually haul brand-new cars, and all we see is one of those. Mostly we pass the big trucks from the chicken plant.

I look in all the parking lots along the way, because it's got to be *some*where, Clara's car. If I drove past the right place, in the right town, I'd see it.

I roll white paint onto the ceiling, a second coat. It sprays white freckles on my arms and cheeks, and I worry that maybe they've painted Clara's car a different color. How will I ever recognize it?

But I hold out some hope. Whenever a little red car goes down our road, my heart pounds so fast. I can't help being disappointed when it's a Toyota or a Chevrolet. I get so mad that I make myself go back to the workshop and use a brush to recoat the windowsills.

I tell myself, *For every time you go looking for red cars, you have to do fifty stomach crunches before bed.* But that doesn't stop me. I think about red cars when I'm doing the crunches.

I don't know what it means that I want a red Pontiac myself, if it's a death wish or maybe something else. If I had a red Pontiac, I might paint it white, but I'd know it was red once, and that'd be all that mattered.

IT'S OCTOBER, AND THERE ARE TREASURES at the beach most every day. I find a float on the rocks beside the pier, a big blue one as long as my body and slightly wider. It must have blown off a yacht passing by, or maybe there was a shipwreck we didn't hear about. In any case, it's two inches thick and the prettiest blue, blue as the sky in July, and firm. It has a built-in pillow, raised up for your head, and one place at the bottom where it looks like maybe a fish took a bite, and a cut place near the top, probably where it hung up on barnacles.

In my mind, I picture Rhonda in a bikini, stretched out on that float, sleeping behind her sunglasses, and I wonder if she's on her honeymoon yet, and hope she's found some peace.

The float isn't heavy, but it's wet, with extra water dripping out the punctures, so I take it home and stand it up in the workshop to drain. It's the right size to be my mattress when I move in. It'll fit along the top of those cabinets, and I'll sleep up there, in case there are rats on the floor.

At the end of the cabinets, there are three drawers, a small one on top, a bigger one in the middle, and a giant one on the bottom. I've already dumped them out and scrubbed them clean, but it takes forever to fit them back in. And there's nothing I hate worse than flimsy drawers. All my life I've had flimsy drawers.

When I pull out the drawers in the dresser I share with Daphne, I have to wiggle and twist and bump them back and forth to coax them in. I don't think it's right that people should have to make deals with wood. Wood should give and slide.

When I put my jeans in the bottom dresser drawer, the plywood breaks out of its groove every time. I have to tap-tap-tap it back in place. So I decide that when I move into the workshop, I'll build a closet somewhere, in some corner. These drawers will never hold my heavy winter clothes, but maybe they'll hold light things, like socks or spaghetti.

I take some hinges, the ones that Daphne found, and I screw the bottoms of the drawers into the sides to reinforce them. But the bottom is weak to begin with, homemade, an old piece of splintered paneling.

There are people who never think of their drawers—Wendy Honeycutt, probably, or even Rhonda. Their cabinets catch and latch, and their drawers slide easy. They don't have to use a bar of soap along the runners to make the drawers go in and out. They don't have to wiggle and bump and lift a thing to make it fit into its hole.

Things should fit in their holes naturally. That's what I think.

A T LUNCH, MS. BRADY (SARASWATI) asks me how much I know about photography. Though I don't know much, she's willing to give me a try. They need a photographer to cover student activities at the Tech Center. Since most members of the yearbook staff are taking classes to earn college credits, they stay at the regular high school all day long. They don't know the first thing about what goes on at the Tech Center.

But I do. And I'm happy to be of use. I'd do anything for Ms. Brady. I know the kind of picture she's looking for al-ready— students working together to wire a circuit, the cosmetology class giving each other haircuts, students learning to be nurse aids moving people from stretchers to beds.

Ms. Brady promises to give me a crash course in camera basics as soon as the camera I need to use comes back in. (One of the teachers took it to France, and I like to think about that, holding a camera that's been all the way to France.) In the meantime, I spend my lunch periods looking at books about photography, and the way photographers use different lenses to capture different things. Even though I don't have a camera to practice with, I like the idea of framing a thing for the world, picking a moment out of all the other moments, and click— there it is. (Or there it *will* be.)

Ms. Brady writes me a letter to take to the main office at the Tech Center. She calls me a correspondent and says I need free access to all the classrooms and time out of classes to do the shots.

Though I don't have a camera yet, I feel different. When my computer teacher finds out, she smiles at me, maybe for the first time ever. While other students are writing up memos, the teacher calls me over to show me a program that lets you enhance pictures, turning color photos to black and white. She illustrates it on a picture of her dog, a fluffy brown one who goes from sultry to sparkly, depending on which enhancement she clicks.

When my automotive repair teacher learns I'm a

photographer for the yearbook, he says, "Good, maybe this year we'll be represented. Last three yearbooks left us out."

"I'll be sure to get your picture in, sir," I tell him.

"You will, will you?"

"Yes, sir," I say.

"Good," he says. "Now get over there and lubricate that chassis."

I WORRY A LOT ABOUT BLEEDING on myself. It'd be a bad thing, to stand up and see blood on the desk chair. It'd be so bad. So I wear a pad all the time, just in case. Sometimes, even when I'm not bleeding, I convince myself I am, and I worry. I pull at the back of my pants to see if I feel them sticking wet, and I can't believe it when I get home and there's nothing there.

I worry about bleeding in the bed. I don't want to bleed at all, don't want Tim-Tim or Quincy to know when it happens, and if I bleed in the bed and Daphne finds out, or Aunt Glo, they might let it slip and then Quincy and Tim-Tim would make fun.

So I sleep in a pad every night, just in case.

Before it really happens, I know, of course, I know—that low aching—and I hurry to the bathroom to check, and sometimes I put a pad up high and low both, so I won't be caught by accident with stained-up pants.

Aunt Glo complains that I use too many, and I do, but I

have to. She only buys one box a month, so I have to save the ones I haven't bled on and use them again. That seems reasonable. I don't blame Aunt Glo for setting a limit. It's not right for me to spend her good money on my neuroses; that's what she says. The government doesn't send her enough to pay for me to waste.

So I roll them up and stash them behind my dresser drawer in case I need backups. I don't know what I'll do when I'm eighteen and have to buy my pads myself. Maybe shop in stores two towns away and make small talk to the clerk about my girlfriend and her PMS.

I wear two pairs of underpants every day, my own and then some that used to belong to my daddy. When he went to prison, he could only have white underwear, so I have his black jockey shorts as a backup layer.

I have a pair of bike shorts, too, made of spandex. They're my favorites. They fit tight and cover me from my middle down nearly to my knees. I wear them beneath my jeans, and I like how tight they are. I like knowing that if anybody held me down and tried to pull my pants off, they'd have a job ahead of them, and if I kicked and screamed, I might make enough racket to get help before they made it through all the layers.

With all the layers, I almost feel like I could bleed and it wouldn't stain my clothes before I had a chance to get to the bathroom. Not all the way through, anyway.

But then I'd have to *go* to the bathroom at school, and that'd be bad.

So even though I hate the blood, and even though I dread it, I pray sometimes to Christjesus during the Morning Devotional (when we've all got our heads bowed and eyes closed) that

I'll get my period on Friday afternoon after school, so the worst of it will be over by Monday.

No matter how prepared I am, when I go to the toilet and wipe and see that smear, I can't stand it. I get dizzy, close my eyes. I tell myself it's good, because soon it will be over, and I won't have to worry about it again for weeks. I close my eyes and try to do visualization, like the art teacher taught us in seventh grade (but she was a wack job), and I picture the clots falling out of me in a strand of black beads.

M s. Brady (Saraswati) knows a man who buys other people's junk and sells it over the Internet. She lets me use the phone in the workroom to call him, and that's how it happens that I sell him the antique oyster tongs, the old sewing machine, the painted dishes, all the odds and ends I've stacked up in the bathroom at the back of the workshop.

"It's in there," I tell him. I don't follow him in. I point the way and act like I'm busy, scraping up bits of linoleum left on the floor, and I hear him bumping around, examining things, the old typewriter, the glasses with frames that wrap around your ears.

He comes out with a notepad, scratches a bill of sale, and loads it all into the back of his truck. I hope that Jarvis Stanley doesn't see and mention it to Aunt Glo. I hope Tim-Tim doesn't see, or Quincy, and I hope the man hurries up and gets away before the bus drops Daphne off, because even though Aunt Glo told me to throw it in the Dumpster, she'd want a cut if she knew I made a hundred and thirty dollars.

I'M TEMPTED TO BUY A CAMERA. If I had a camera, and if I got good at taking pictures, I could be a photographer, maybe for weddings, or maybe even for the newspaper. Then everybody'd leave me alone because I'd be an artist, and artists can get away with anything. They can wear berets in the summertime if they want to.

I'm tempted to take my hundred and thirty dollars and buy a bus ticket to Georgia. Maybe I'd find Rhonda. I picture her running up to hug me and thanking me for taking such good care of her the night Jarvis Stanley tried to kill her. She'd want to introduce me to everybody in town. Maybe Rhonda'd take me to the bar where my momma played guitar, and they'd all remember her there. They'd really miss her.

Maybe Clara Tinsley's parents would be there, too, and they'd want to give me something in appreciation. Even though I didn't do anything to save Clara Tinsley, I don't let that stop my fantasy. In my fantasy, they want me to have her little red Pontiac. I cash in my bus ticket for gas money and drive it home. (In my fantasy, I know how to drive, even though Aunt Glo says I'm too high-strung and can learn later, when I settle down.) I stop in to see my granny, who's sorry she wasn't able to provide a home when my daddy went to prison, and I forgive her, tell her not to ever think about it again. I've been just fine.

But when I measure my dollars against my daydreams, I can't justify a bus ticket or a camera, either one. So instead, I spend my money on ceramic tiles.

The workshop needs a new floor, and Wendy agrees to take me to the Home Emporium, where they have tiles for sixty cents apiece. They're not pretty tiles—not colored ones like I'd pick if I had all the money in the world, green or blue or even red—but basic beige tiles. I'm hoping to ride in Wendy's new Camaro, but when she picks me up, she's driving one of her daddy's trucks, a small one with gears that she keeps fighting. We jerk down the street and cut off at a stop sign, but she cranks it right back up.

"Thank you," I tell her. "The tiles are too heavy to carry on the bus."

"No problem," she says. "I need an organizer for my closet anyway."

Later, she asks me why Aunt Glo couldn't drive me to Home Emporium, and I tell her that I'm fixing up the workshop on the sly and don't want Aunt Glo to see it before it's done. It's a lie, but one that makes her admire me.

"That's so sweet of you," she says, and I blush.

She asks me if I know how to do tiles, and I tell her I checked out a book about it from the library, and Wendy compliments me on how good I am with my hands.

I walk through the Home Emporium with Wendy, and the sales associates nod and don't pay us any attention. When I'm with Wendy, I don't attract attention, and it makes me happy to think that people glance at us and imagine we're a couple.

Wendy's curls roll around her back as she pushes her cart along the concrete floors, and I follow, happy to be out where nobody knows me, looking at closet organizers. But then she says, "Kenny, why don't you get your tiles, and I'll meet you up front."

"Oh," I say. "Okay, sure." I'm not sure if she's trying to save time or if she doesn't want to be seen with me, but I try not to act too sheepish about it.

The tiles come eleven to a box and look like they're made of pale clay. I do the math in my head and decide I need twelve boxes, and there's no way that many will fit into a cart, and they're too heavy to heave inside it anyway. So I get a flatbed wagon and load it up and hope I have enough money. I'd forgotten about the mortar, the grout, and the spacers.

The sales associate who helps me load my cart acts suspicious of me and my project. "You're tiling a workshop?"

"Yes, sir," I tell him.

"What for?" he asks.

"In case it floods again," I say.

"Huh," he says and throws the mortar on top of the heap. "You'll need one of these."

He pulls a trowel off a shelf, but I tell him I've got one and push as hard as I can to get that flatbed to the cashier. It doesn't turn very easy, and I knock over a display of batteries, just what I need. When I bend to pick them up, my ball cap comes off. I know it leaves a ledge around my head, so I ruffle my hair really quick so I won't look like a loser. Everybody's looking at me.

But Wendy hurries to help. She's laughing. "Goodness gracious," she exclaims. "Look how many there are!" She's talking about tiles, not batteries, and it's so ridiculous, this load I'm pushing around, that I start laughing, too. She's already checked out and put her closet organizer in the truck, so she waits with me in the checkout line, and it takes almost all my money, but I have enough.

"Not enough to get lunch on the way home, though."

"I'm not hungry," I tell her. "Go ahead and eat."

She gets me a water and orders a big side of french fries to go, and we sit in her daddy's truck and share them.

"I've been wanting to talk to you," she says.

"You have?"

"Yeah," she says. "I just want you to know—" And she chokes up.

It's not like Wendy to do that. Wendy's the kind of girl whose words pour easy as cupcake batter. So I get scared, like I do when something I'm not expecting happens, like the first time I found out my daddy was in jail and I ran to the old carnival grounds and hid until dark. I think for sure Wendy's got cancer.

"I might not understand your lifestyle," she says. "And it might go against my personal beliefs—but I don't believe in judging, either."

"Okay," I say, and I'm still trying to figure out exactly what she means.

"A lot of people would say you belong in hell," she continues. "And for a while now, since you've been coming to Morning Devotional, I've been praying you'll change. But I'm not doing that anymore, Kenny. I'm going to pray for you to live out God's will for your life."

"Oh," I tell her. My face is so hot, the heat flushing up my neck. "Okay." I wonder if she's expecting me to say "thank you," but before I have a chance to say anything, she leans over and gives me a hug, the most awkward hug in the world, with seat belts in the way and her hair boinging in my mouth, and two quick pat-pats on my back, and then she pulls away.

Eighth grade, when we were in PE class together, the year before I cut off my hair and started binding myself up, Wendy confided to me that she was constipated. We were doing sit-ups, and I was holding her feet, and her face was all twisted and red-splotched as she rose from the floor. She let out a big breath and hunkered there over her knees, and she whispered it to me when the gym teacher wasn't looking. She said it was the very worst thing, to have your period and be constipated at the same time.

I thought then that she was my best friend, because who else would tell you something like that? I hadn't really considered it before, but I believed her the minute she said it.

Ever since, I've wondered about it, wondered how she came up with such a thing as her very worst predicament. I've wondered why she told me.

"I may not understand," she tells me now. "But I won't stop praying for you."

I just nod because I don't know what else to do, and she throws the truck in gear, and we jerk back to Aunt Glo's, where Wendy ties her blond curls back and heaves out tiles by my side.

I KICK ALONG THE BEACH and think about my lifestyle. I didn't know I *had* one, and truth be told, I sort of thought you had to be eighteen to qualify. I'm surprised that Wendy doesn't agree with my lifestyle, because that implies I've chosen to live a certain way when I haven't really chosen anything at all.

The sand doesn't choose to mound up in a particular place. It just lands there grain by grain. Other forces—the wind, the geography, the toes of my sneakers—determine where the peaks and valleys happen. I sit down on some sand and flatten it against the earth. It's not a lifestyle. It's my *ass* on the sand, crushing it down. Who asked Wendy if she understood my lifestyle? And what is it about me that offends her so much, anyway?

A crab scuttles sideways. That isn't a choice. It runs from the black dog that chases it along the beach. You can't say the crab's got a fast-paced lifestyle because it runs. You can't say the crab's high-strung. The dog's after it. That's all.

Does a dog have a lifestyle? When it runs along mudflats and makes the seagulls scatter, is that a lifestyle or what a dog's instincts tell it to do?

It's windy, and my cheeks sting tight, and I keep replaying Wendy Honeycutt's voice, all concerned and prissy, saying she doesn't agree with my lifestyle. But she doesn't judge (or so she says), like *some* people who think I'm going to hell.

Does a jellyfish belong in hell because it stings some-body swimming? I don't believe in hell, not really, but if I did, I wouldn't expect to go there.

I get a sick feeling, thinking that maybe somehow Wendy Honeycutt found out that a long time ago I let Daphne suck my titties. If I belong in hell, I know that's why. Maybe there's some sign, some secret smell that I don't know about, something to caution other people that I'm a bad person.

Then I just get mad again, because there's *no* way, because I was trying to get rid of cancer, because *what does Wendy Honeycutt know about me?*

Before I dressed like a boy, back when I dressed like a girl, Tim-Tim wanted to practice with me all the time. First just kiss-ing, then rubbing, then thrusting, just to see what it felt like. It wasn't a lifestyle for him to want to practice. It wasn't even wrong. I wasn't his sister, not really.

It wasn't a lifestyle for me to want him to stop. "But I *did* want him to stop. I didn't want it on the rusted Tilt-A-Whirl down at the old carnival grounds. I didn't want it in the bath-room when Aunt Glo was still at work. I didn't want it behind the Armory, under the pier, outside the jail, beneath a little cata-maran somebody left on the beach.

So I cut my hair, bound my tits, layered my pants, turned into a boy. If Tim-Tim wouldn't stop, then I'd make him a queer. Just that easy.

Not a lifestyle. Just a life. Just *my* life.

W E'RE ALL SITTING AROUND THE TABLE, finishing up Sunday dinner, which Aunt Glo serves in the afternoon, and we're making small talk with Tim-Tim's new girlfriend, a girl with thick black eyeliner and a curly dark permanent who's told us to call her Sneaky, when shadows cross over the leftover biscuits and settle onto the pecan pie. Aunt Glo pushes back in her chair and leans toward the window. "Somebody's out in the yard taking pictures," she declares.

"Who is it?" asks Tim-Tim, and by then we've all gotten up to see.

"Rental lady," Quincy says. "Wonder what she wants?"

We follow Aunt Glo outside, and the rental lady clicks a few more frames before she looks at us. She's sappy sweet when she says, "Hi. How are *you?*" She's in a business suit, a tailored skirt just above her knees, a matching jacket, and though it's Sunday, it doesn't look like the kind of outfit she might have worn to church. She looks like an airplane stewardess, and she's wearing panty hose. The minute I see them, I get a charge all through me.

Tim-Tim lowers his voice when he asks, "What are you doing?"

"Oh," she says, "I'm getting some photos for my lawyer." She looks at where she's standing, which is right in the middle of our front lawn. "I'm not trespassing," she proclaims, even though technically she is. "Don't call the police."

Nobody was about to call the police, but we don't get time to tell her this before she starts throwing her hands around, saying, "The last thing I need is more trouble. That girl's family, the Tinsleys, they've filed a lawsuit. A civil suit." She sighs hard and shakes her head, and I feel exhilarated—and also a little bit sorry for her.

"What's a civil suit?" Daphne asks me. She's leaped up into the porch swing, and I give her a push and tell her to shhh.

Aunt Glo nods and asks, "So why are you taking pictures of *our* house?"

"Well," she says, "my lawyer wanted to get a sense of the place—where it happened."

"What's a civil suit?" Daphne insists, and I hop in the swing beside her and elbow her good. We make room for Sneaky, who joins us there while Tim-Tim stands with Aunt Glo and Quincy leans on a porch rail behind.

Tim-Tim's trying to impress his new girl, I can tell; he talks right on that edge of harsh politeness. I listen because I want to be able to talk like that, not scared, not always accommodating. I hate how my voice sounds even when I talk low and quiet like I do. Aunt Glo's a grown woman, but she's still got those girl-ish ways about her, trying to make everybody comfortable, even her enemies. She laughs when the rental lady points out that our house looks lived in, like a permanent residence, while hers (she points across the street) looks like a rental. It even has a name, the Beachcomber, painted on a plaque up high along the porch roof. So it makes perfect sense that *that* house would be the rental, while Jarvis Stanley's, with its broken chair and full spittoon, would not.

"See here," Tim-Tim says to the rental lady. "We've got nothing against you personally. But what happened with that girl was an abomination." He says that. "Abomination." I know he must have heard it said that way, or maybe read it in the paper, and I wonder if Sneaky knows the word. "So we'd all appreciate it if you'd finish up with your pictures and go."

"I'll do that," the rental lady agrees, and we're about to go in and finish dessert when Jarvis Stanley stumbles out his front door. He's had a hard night of drinking, and one eye looks at the rental lady while the other eye looks at us.

"Whatsamatter?" he asks. You can tell he's not quite sure who the rental lady is.

"It's all right," Tim-Tim says. "She's done."

Jarvis figures it out. "Get off this property," he slurs. "You don't belong here."

But the rental lady doesn't just listen when a man says "boo!" I want to be like that, too. I picture myself with her camera, taking the kinds of pictures that cause regimes to fall, that cause spies to be deployed to steal the film and keep their secrets secret.

The rental lady backs onto the sidewalk and says, "There you go. I'm on public property now. I have every right to be here."

"You ought to be tried and hanged," Jarvis declares. "Do you know what this has done to my reputation? And *you* the one who caused it."

"It was a misunderstanding," she says, but she doesn't seem too sorry about it.

"Least you coulda done was paid for the cleanup."

"I'm the one being sued," the rental lady says. "For a million dollars. It'll cost me fifty grand in attorney fees even if they drop the charges, and you want me to pay to have your *house* cleaned? I didn't tell you to shoot her!"

"All righty now," Tim-Tim says. "You better go."

So the rental lady stomps off Nothing gets to her. Aunt Glo invites Jarvis over to have some pie and meet Sneaky, and he agrees to come, and that's almost enough reason for me to help the rental lady with her yard—but not quite. When she calls across the way, "Hey, Kenny? Can you help me mulch the shrubs this afternoon?" I say, "Sorry, ma'am. I've got homework."

It almost feels good to say no, even though I could have used another ten dollars and even though not helping means I have to sit around the table with Jarvis.

But Jarvis stays away from me. He liked me better when I was little. He listens to the story of how Sneaky and her momma had just moved to town, and on the first cold night, their heater wouldn't work. Tim-Tim was the one sent to check on things, and he discovered that they had the thermostat turned to emergency heat instead of regular; there was nothing wrong with the heater at all. Everybody laughs.

Jarvis asks Daphne to sit in his lap, so he can "ridey horsey" with her, but she says, "Shit no! I'm too old for that."

Aunt Glo says, "Daphne!"

But Daphne's not done. "Besides that," she says, "you smell like whiskey, and I don't want you getting it on my new shirt."

Aunt Glo's about to fuss, but Jarvis just laughs and says, "It's all right, Gloria. I like 'em feisty."

Later on, me and Quincy and Daphne and Tim-Tim and Sneaky all go out into the yard, and Quincy's friend Roger comes over and evens out the teams, and we play football in the grass. I tackle Tim-Tim, and Sneaky laughs. I tackle Sneaky, and

Tim-Tim says, "Easy, now," but Sneaky seems to like it. She lays beneath me giggling and winded, then holds tight to my hand when I help her up. Even though I intended to tile the workshop today, it doesn't seem like such a big deal to wait.

W HEN I OPEN UP THE BOXES OF TILES, some of them are broken. They *came* that way, and I can't believe it. Some have cracked midway through, and some have the tips chipped off, almost whole, almost perfect, but ruined anyway. I yell when I see them. "Dammit!" I yell, because can't *anything* be easy for me? How will I get more?

But after I lay out the tiles, I see that I'll need the broken pieces to work around the edges, where whole pieces wouldn't fit. Even if it's not perfect, it'll be better than it is now.

I might have a questionable lifestyle, but at least I have some *skills*.

So I start. I follow the directions from the book, measuring and tacking a string right through the middle of the floor. I make a grid. It takes a long time. Tiling a floor is such slow work. It takes me all of October.

My fingers bleed, all cut up on those tiles. They drip onto the clay, but I don't care. It makes me feel real. If I have blood, I must be real. I drip my blood signature onto that floor, **KENNY WAS HERE,** without even needing any words.

The sales associate at Home Emporium warned me that there are tiny pieces of glass inside the mortar that can cut your lungs to bits and choke you near to death. So I'm careful mixing it up and try not to breathe the powder that poofs up everywhere. I mix it with water. I stir and stir till my arms are sore, and I use kitchen gloves to squeeze the big lumps out.

I pretend to have special powers, to fight cancer with my gloved hands, breaking up lumps, smoothing them, blending them in, and I think of my momma up in heaven (except I don't really believe in heaven) looking down on me and knowing it was worth it, her cancer, her dying, because now I can cure it for anybody at all, and I discovered the secret by breaking up lumps in mortar. I tell myself that cancer's nothing but a dry patch of something that's supposed to be wet.

I like spreading mortar, and if I don't become an armored car delivery guard, I can be a bricklayer. I use the trowel Aunt Glo saved from the things I took to the dump, her daddy's old trowel. It's got a wooden handle, not a metal one like the one at Home Emporium, and it's shaped different. But it works to lift and plop the gray mud onto the concrete floor. I slap it down and spread it out, easy as icing a cake. Maybe I can be a baker, a pastry chef I plunk tiles onto the mortared floor, one after the next.

The spacers look like grave markers, tiny crosses standing up across a field of tiles. I try to use them to keep the tiles lined straight, but the gaps widen in spite of everything. I hunker into spaces I have to back out of, and when I use up a batch of mortar and quit for the day, the muscles in the backs of my legs are stretched and achy, and my lower back hurts in a way that I know even a hot bath won't help.

In my sleep, I tile the floor. I think of straight lines and grave markers, my momma's grave that I haven't seen in how many years? I count them. Nine. And before that, I only saw her grave a time or two, on her birthday when Daddy and I took flowers, back before we moved. Her grave was always in the sunshine. The sunshine bleached the plastic flowers to the color of clay.

In my sleep, I follow streets of mortar, a grid of streets, a gravestone at every crossing, and I can't find my momma's grave anymore. They all look the same.

It's the worst night's sleep I've ever had, so here's the crazy thing: I forget to wake up at two to drink my water. Now it's morning, and I'm parched. I have to drink a little, but I don't want to pee at school.

I tell Aunt Glo, "I'm staying home," because maybe this lower-back pain means my period's coming early, and what if I start it there?

Aunt Glo says, "Get your ass on that bus."

So I do.

INSTEAD OF GOING TO MORNING DEVOTIONAL, I sit in a corner of the Commons Area and read a book, and that works out okay. I don't want to see Wendy. I don't know what to say.

It might be psychological, but it seems like by nine o'clock, I already have to pee. By ten o'clock, all my guts are floating, and worse than that, I think I might cry, because I try so hard, *so hard,* to make my life livable. Then one little thing goes wrong and it all falls apart.

I have to pee so bad it feels like I've got thorns between my legs. I could go to the Guidance Office if I wanted to. Last year a guidance counselor pulled me out of class to tell me she'd heard I didn't use the school bathrooms. (Ms. Brady must have told— or maybe Wendy Honeycutt.) This guidance counselor said if it became a problem, they had a unisex bathroom I could use.

But if I went there, I'd have to sign in and explain it to the receptionist. And after that, the guidance counselor'd want to talk. She'd be listening for the flush, waiting to ask me why I didn't use the regular bathroom.

So when the bell rings and everybody's changing classes, I leave. I walk right out the side door, the one beside the physical science lab that says, **EMERGENCY EXIT ONLY,** and nobody stops me. No alarms go off! I walk right off the grounds, and nothing happens at all.

There are woods beside the high school. When I was in ninth grade, we did Project Adventure there and blindfolded each other and led each other through the trees by the sounds of our voices. Wendy was my partner for that, too.

I follow the same trails deep into the woods, and when I'm sure there are no PE classes out, I squat against a pine and empty my bladder, and oh my God, it's good. If I get red bugs, it'll be worth it. I pee like the world's coming to an end. I pee like I was born to do nothing else.

I don't know how long it takes to walk home. It's at least five miles, and I wish I'd left some of my books in my locker, but I don't use it because people put things through the slats— eyeballs from the frogs they dissect in lab or turdy toilet paper—and I don't want that nastiness on my books.

I still have my banana, and I have my apple, so I eat lunch. I walk right along the highway through tall grasses and potato-chip bags, and after a while, Miss Mattie from down the street passes by and stops. She's been to the grocery store and is on her way home, and what in the world am I doing? I tell her I missed the bus for the Tech Center, the one I usually catch after lunch.

So that's how I get home in time to work on my tiles.

M Y MORTAR IS MIXED IN A BIG enamel pot that makes an awful screech when I drag it over the floor. Daphne covers her ears and sometimes her dolls' ears. She hangs out with me when I work, and when I'm not paying attention, she sneaks some mortar to give her dolls spa treatments. She saw spa treatments on television, so she puts mud on their faces. I wouldn't care, except it's not free—mortar. It's gonna take all I've got and more to finish this floor.

"Don't you have some homework to do?" I ask her.

"Did it at Resource," she says.

She gets braver and lets her dolls sit on the edge of my enamel pot and soak their feet and legs. I upend one with my trowel, and the doll falls backward in the mortar I've just spread.

"Hey! Now I'm gonna have to wash her hair," Daphne complains.

"Tough," I say. "Go do it."

"You old poop-tart," she grumbles under her breath, but she takes her dolls and leaves.

Once again, I'm working until my batch of mortar's all used up. My hands are red and achy, and the tile cuts are inflamed by the sandy mortar. I'm wearing gloves, but when I wash them off—and I have to wash them off anytime I do something else, like get Daphne some crackers, stick the hen in the oven and set the timer, blow my nose—water gets inside them. So my hands stay slightly wet and slightly raw all the time.

So my hands are aching, and my back's aching, too, and I'm wondering if anybody at school will notice I didn't go to economics. I didn't turn in my practice 1040EZ (even though I did a pretty good job configuring my withholdings), didn't board the bus to the Tech Center, didn't show up for computer class or automotive repair. I finish up for the day and go to hose off the enamel pot, and what do I find? Daphne playing hopscotch on my good tiles right there in the yard—they *used* to be good tiles—with Quincy and Roger goading her on and laughing.

"What are you doing?" I shout.

"What does it look like I'm doing?" Daphne sasses. She looks like a puppet, with so many missing teeth. She throws her quarter onto a tile way up toward the end of the line. And it's a long line. There must be twenty lines of tiles, some single, some double. She takes off, hop, hop, hop, and I can hear them, crack, crack, crack, and I go after her.

"You little shit!" I holler. "I'm gonna kill you," and I chase her out of the yard, and I've almost got her when Quincy yells,

"Run!" When I stop to look back, he and Roger are doubled over, whinnying. They can't even breathe, they're laughing so hard.

"Why didn't you stop her?" I shout at them, and I must look fierce because Roger hops over the fence and Quincy's right behind him. It's a low fence anyway, and leaning, so it's nothing. They hop right across.

Daphne has darted into Jarvis Stanley's yard, screaming "Help" as loud as she can. She trips over his water hose and hurts her knee. I can see it starting to bleed as she bangs on his door, calling, "Save me! Kenny's gone kill me!"

Jarvis opens it right before I get there. "What in God's name?" he says. He pulls her into his house, huddles her to him. Then I'm standing there on the stoop with the screen door between us, and Daphne's wailing like I've beat her to a bloody pulp, even though I haven't laid a finger on her.

"Back off!" he hollers at me. He opens the door fast and knocks me off the stoop with it. I stumble back into his holly tree. "She's half your size!"

"She broke my tiles," I say. I wave my dirty yellow gloves around and try to make him understand.

"Don't make no difference," he says. Then: "You wait till Gloria gets home."

She'll be mad. I know how mad she'll be. 'Cause Daphne's her grandbaby—and the only thing in this world that keeps her attached to her firstborn, Constance. And I'm nothing. Nobody.

A nobody with a lifestyle.

I wash off Daphne's dolls and do my best to get the mortar out of their eyes. But some of it's dried on there for good.

A T LEAST THE WALLS ARE THIN. While I'm taking the chicken out of the oven and heating up the canned green beans, I can hear Daphne talking to Jarvis. I can hear everything she says. "How come you look like an old platterpus?" she asks him.

"Well, now," he says. "I don't rightly know."

"Was your daddy an old platterpus?" she asks, and she giggles.

"Maybe so," Jarvis said. "I didn't know him."

"Don't feel bad," Daphne says. "I don't know my daddy or momma neither one." I sure hope she hasn't hopped into his lap to pet his cheeks the way she does mine when I'm feeling low, because Jarvis has that "ridey horsey" tendency, and Daphne's too little to understand.

She asks him for some paper, and he gives her an old brown sack. I know this because she says, "Don't you got any white paper?" and he says, "I might have the back of an envelope," and she says, "I'll just draw on this bag then." She adds, "This is what a platterpus looks like."

Aunt Glo will be home any minute, and she'll be tired when she gets here. She worked a double, and even if all she does is refill Pepsis and flip burgers, that's a lot when you're forty-five and have bunions.

I'm tempted to leave before she gets home, except I don't want to leave Daphne with Jarvis. Nobody's going to be able to accuse me of not being there for her, even if she's so scared of me she'd rather spend her evening with a *known murderer.*

How offensive is *that?*

Quincy's eating at Roger's house, and Tim-Tim's eating at Sneaky's, so there's nobody but me there when Aunt Glo gets home. I cut her off on the porch and say, "We had a fight. Daphne's with Jarvis."

"What?" she says. I hear her voice getting panicked. "What kind of fight? What happened?" She's already crossed over to Jarvis's porch and is banging at the door. So I take off.

"Kenny!" she hollers at me, but then somebody opens the door, and I'm too far down the street for her to see me anyway. "Kenny!" she calls again, but it's past dark, and I keep on going. 'Cause if I owe myself anything, it's the chance for Aunt Glo to calm down after Jarvis accuses me of whatever he's got planned. I can hear him now: "That gal's got problems!" That's what he'll say. "You ought to turn her over to the state." He's said it all before. This time Aunt Glo just might listen.

So I don't go to the beach. That'd be the first place she'd look if she came out there to whip me. If Daphne says I threatened to kill her, if Aunt Glo believes it, she might even call the police. Maybe it's a crime to threaten a minor. I cut back around the next block and walk the other way, down to the old carnival grounds, where there hasn't been a carnival since I moved to Virginia. It's not the safest place to be because people who do drugs buy them behind the toppled-over Ferris wheel. It has brown grass growing up tall between the spikes, and the seats are all missing.

Sometimes drug dealers do their business behind the base, which looks like a rusty metal wall.

But what do I care about being safe? What difference would it make if somebody kicked my teeth out? At least if they put me in the hospital, I'd have somewhere to spend the night.

I'm not scared of drug dealers; I know them all anyway. But I stay away from the Ferris wheel just the same. There's a bench off to the side of the bumper cars that I go sit on. The bumper cars are inside a fence, but you can get right in. Somebody's cut the fence in two or three places and pushed the wire back. I don't know why anyone would want to sit in an old bumper car, knowing it's where wildcats and raccoons live year-round, and snakes in the summertime. Most of the cars are on their sides, cracked and battered.

It's all I can do not to cry, but I'm too mad to cry, because I don't deserve this. I *don't*. I don't know how Daphne could do it to me—break my tiles on purpose and then run screaming to the likes of Jarvis Stanley. And knowing he shot a girl's head off! Now Aunt Glo might not want me back.

My eyes get wet and the bumper cars go blurry. I try to make myself feel better by thinking about Rhonda. She didn't deserve what she got, either, but that didn't stop her from going on with her life. Maybe she's married by now. Maybe her husband moved her to Missouri and she's forgotten about the day she watched her best friend's brains dripping off of Jarvis Stan-ley's lamp shade.

(How could Daphne go in his house?)

I hunker down inside my coat and stare at the old bumper cars until one of them seems to move, and I tense up and stare harder, but nothing happens. I tell myself it's the wind blowing the air between my eyes and that bumper car around; it's an illusion. But I'm spooked. Then I start thinking there might be other dead girls stuffed inside old bumper cars—not just here but on carnival grounds everywhere, all across America.

Seems like I can't stop my mind, so I'm actually grateful when I see a bulldog over by the Tilt-A-Whirl, where, on warmer nights, the scallop shells hide lovers making out on busted seats. I see the dog, and the dog sees me, and he stops and looks square at me, considering.

If he charges, I'll charge him, too, run right up on him and fight him till the death. What difference would it make if he ate me alive? I wouldn't care.

But the dog goes the other way.

My knees are shaking. I can't stop them. They do a little better when I walk, so I head back to the beach.

I CROUCH BENEATH THE PIER between some rocks and wait out the moon. It climbs up and up and up—I can see it through the cracks in the boards—and I close my eyes and try to sleep. But a rock butts into my back, and another one nudges wrong against my neck. When I move to a comfortable position, I'm in the wind again. I should have brought my earmuffs. It's November now, and you need earmuffs sometimes in November.

I pull myself into a ball, my hands between my thighs, huddle my face down into the collar of my coat, and try to be all right. But I feel crazy in my head, so crazy. I don't know why I'm trying to keep my skin out of the cold. I don't care if I get frostbite. I *hate* my body. I am 50 *sick* of living in my body.

Maybe I doze off a little, I must, because my daddy comes to see me there beneath the pier.

The last time I saw him, he was already incarcerated. We'd driven a long way, six hours. He had a crew cut and he was reddish tan, even though he complained about not being able to go outside very much. His skin was burned, but that was only because they didn't have shade out in the yard, and there was nowhere for him to buy sunscreen. I couldn't stand to look at his sad red face, so I looked at his arms. The blond hairs on his arms made his blurry tattoos even blurrier.

Tonight he looks different, empty as a cartoon. Maybe he got brainwashed stupid in prison.

"Did you break out?" I ask him.

"No," he says. "You can't break out."

But I know it's possible. I've seen the news—people break out. But my daddy's a spineless coward. He doesn't have the nerve. Maybe he doesn't even want to. If he wasn't in prison, he'd have to take care of me. Suddenly I realize his life might be easier in prison. All this time I've been worried about him. It makes me so mad.

"Well, what are you doing here, then?" I ask him.

"I don't know," he says. He looks around like he doesn't recognize this place, even though we've fished here together a hundred times. "I was just wandering by, I guess."

Maybe he doesn't recognize me. Maybe he thinks I'm some homeless boy.

Then he wanders away. He climbs over rocks, crawls along them on his hands and knees, and I can see that he's not my real daddy. If he was my real daddy, he'd raise hell because I cut my hair so short, and when he did, I'd say, "Go fuck yourself, Greg Lugo." I wouldn't even call him "Daddy." "You got no right to tell me how to fix my hair. *You* left *me.*"

But this is just a daddy drawn onto a paper bag. When he falls off the rocks and into the bay, he'll float away like a map. Now I'm awake for sure, wondering if Daphne's sleeping and what's happening in *her* dreams.

I CAN'T STAND TO THINK OF LOSING DAPHNE. It makes me want to do something crazy, like bang my head into this rock, and so I do it a time or two, and it seems to help. At least it gets rid of the other thoughts, so I whack my head again. But I can't make myself do it very hard. I feel to see if I'm bleeding, but my fingers are too cold to tell.

I don't cry, though. If I freeze to death, I don't want to be found with tear icicles and snot glazed on my lips.

I nudge into the sand a little deeper and try to go to sleep and get it over with. Either I'll freeze or I won't. I close my eyes, but it's almost like they're still open, and in my mind, I'm walking along the beach at low tide. When the tide recedes, the motion leaves curved ridges in the sand. Like a lunar land-scape—we studied those in physical science—or like the roof of your mouth. When it's cold, like tonight, the bits of trapped water freeze inside those ridges.

Don't ask me why I start to think of Daphne dead, but I do. I picture the roof of her mouth (which is easy to see, given all her missing teeth) completely frozen. Her spit clouds solid in the ridges of her palate. She must have wandered off in the night to look for me, and that's how she froze, out there in her penguin pajamas and no shoes, and won't Aunt Glo be mad now. She'll be mad at me forever.

I knock my head into the rock again and tell myself to stop it, and I wish somebody would come kill me, because I'm spineless like my daddy and too much of a coward to kill myself.

Poor Kenny, I hear my momma say. It settles me when I hear her voice. I'd forgotten her voice. *Poor Kenny.* I hope she's coming for me, like they say happens when you die and the dead return to show you the way. *Poor Kenny,* she whispers, but I can't picture her at all, and then I realize it's not a human voice I'm hearing. It's the wind leaning into the sign that warns you not to climb on the rocks.

It strikes me funny when I figure that out. I'm too unlucky to die, and now in addition to these fingers I can't bend, these cheeks I can't feel, I've got a throbbing head from where I gave myself a whipping I deserved. I laugh right out loud in the middle of the night. I exaggerate it, "Ha ha ha ha," as loud as I can holler. (That way, if Daphne really has come out looking for me, she'll hear me and climb down into these rocks before she freezes.) I laugh through my shivers. I put my face inside my shirt and ha-ha-ha hot air onto my chest until my laughing's done.

I must doze off again, or else I sleepwalk back to the carnival grounds, because the next thing I know, I'm riding bumper cars with Rhonda, and with Clara Tinsley, whose face is blown off. Rhonda makes goofy faces at me when I ram my car into hers, but it's hard to tell how Clara feels, since she only has half an expression, and Ms. Brady (Saraswati) has a bumper car, too, but hers is stuck against the wall, grinding against itself, and she can't back up. She doesn't seem to notice that she's not going anywhere. She's enjoying herself just the same.

Then there's a woman I've never seen before, and her bumper car's out of control. She's spinning that wheel to the left and the right, but it seems like the way she steers has nothing to do with where she winds up. All at once I know who she is: Irene Earle, the woman whose prescription Aunt Glo keeps taking.

She needs her medicine back.

WHEN THE SUN COMES UP, I'm still alive. I climb out from my hiding place, stretch my stove-up muscles, and walk out to the end of the pier, where buffleheads swim so peaceful, males and females both. The males look like they should be females, with their pretty white nurses' caps. If I could be a bufflehead, I wouldn't even care if I was male or female. I'd just fly around right over the water like a windup toy, and when I got tired, I'd land on the surface and let the bay float me wherever it wanted.

The winds have died down, and I'm so tired. The bay is perfectly calm, perfectly flat, and I wish I could lay my head on it and float off into eternity. It looks *that* soft. I'm almost in a trance when Tim-Tim shows up. First I feel the boards beneath me vibrating, and when I turn around, I see him coming this way. But I don't go meet him. He might be mad, too. He's got his toboggan cap pulled hard down over his head, his coveralls on. His breath reaches me a few seconds before he does. "Damn Almighty," he says. "You been out here all night?"

"No," I say.

"I know it," he reports. "'Cause I came looking for you."

And I'm secretly pleased to hear it, but I wonder why he asked.

We stand out there together, me and Tim-Tim, like old times. I'm too stiff to move, so I watch the buffles swimming in their clusters. He points at the birds. "Looks like they're being followed by 'greater than/less than' signs," he says, and sure enough, the water behind each buffle ripples an arrow.

"I never could get that straight," I tell him. "Which way you pointed it for 'greater than' and which way you pointed it for 'less than.'"

"Don't matter," he says. "It's nothing you'll use in the real world." Then he asks me, "Where'd you sleep?"

I don't look at him. I just shrug.

"Come on," he says. "Momma's worried to death."

I'm crying by then, right there with Tim-Tim, and he doesn't know what to do with me. So he pulls me into a quick hug, then pushes me back, makes a fist, and hits me hard on the shoulder, like we're buddies. "Come on," he says again and leads me home.

*   *   *

Turns out Daphne squalled all night and wouldn't even sleep in her own bed. She's sorry her dolls skanked up my mortar, she says. She's sorry she broke my tiles. She buries her face into my collar, and I hold on. Her head smells like pizza, a warm smell. We're both on the couch, wrapped up in an afghan. I'm shivering beneath Daphne, but I'm clinging to her, too, while Aunt Glo runs me a bath.

Nobody's especially mad at me, or maybe my brain's too frosty to know it. I don't mind when Aunt Glo helps me out of my coat, out of my sweatshirt, out of my pants. I ask for privacy after that, but I can't even get my own socks off, because my fingers won't bend. So I sit on the side of the tub, and Aunt Glo peels them from my cold white feet.

I hold my face down when she takes off my shirt. "Oh, honey," she says, the T-shirt beneath, the bandages, the panty hose under that. I'm shivering too hard to talk, and when I try, I sound ridiculous. So I let her help me out of the bike shorts, the jockeys, the girl briefs beneath. I let her ease me into the tub and I kind of laugh along when she says, "Ironic, ain't it? The parts of your body you hate the most are the parts you protected from the weather the best."

She sits on the tub beside me. She's still in her nightgown, a long pink silky-looking thing, and she's drenched, too, from helping me into the tub. I can see her titties as plain as if she was naked, but she's washing me, saying, "Why in the world, Ken?" and she's sponging easy at the banged place on my head, and dipping her rag back into the hot water, pulling it up to my neck and squeezing so it trickles warm over the scales and sores on my chest.

But I can't talk yet, and when I do, what leaves my mouth isn't what I intend to say. "What's gonna happen when I turn eighteen?" I blurt out too loud, and then I'm wailing. It's embarrassing how loud I am. I hear it, but I can't shut up. And Daphne, who's been sitting on the toilet and watching us, starts snubbing quiet, holding in her cries, maybe to balance me out.

"Nothing special, I don't reckon," Aunt Glo says.

I stammer, "But where will I go?" Still too loud. I can't look at her. I look at my toes.

Aunt Glo says, "Nowhere, baby, unless you want to." My toes are dead-fish white from the knuckle bones up, but the feeling's coming back, and oh, do they throb. "I thought you were gonna kick me out," I say.

Aunt Glo's reached the end of her tenderness. That's her way. "Well, that's the stupidest thing I ever heard, Kenny," she spits. Daphne giggles. "I didn't kick Tim-Tim out when *he* turned eighteen."

"But he's your boy," I say.

"Well, you're my girl," she says. "At least you *used* to be."

"No," I say. "Daphne's your girl."

"Oh, quit feeling sorry for yourself," Aunt Glo says. "It ain't your place to put limits on my love. I've had you near as long as I've had Daphne."

Somehow I hadn't thought of it that way, that she might feel as attached to me as I feel to Daphne—or to her.

WE ALL STAY HOME, me and Daphne and Aunt Glo. Quincy spent the night with Roger, so he missed all the drama. We lay in Aunt Glo's bed and watch game shows, then soap operas, and they tend to me, bring me soup and hot water with vinegar in it, to improve my disposition, Aunt Glo says.

According to her, relationships go through changes every seven years. I've been living with her seven years now, so it's no surprise we're in this funny place.

All afternoon I fade in and out of sleep, and it feels good to be buried under the covers, safe and dreamy. But I keep thinking about buffleheads, and how arrows follow them wherever they go. I wonder if the air behind me points in that way (except I can't see it because it's air). For a little while, I think that maybe the way I'm heading is exactly the way I should.

Part THREE

THAT FEELING LASTS EXACTLY ONE NIGHT, because the next day, three things happen. Tim-Tim wakes us up early, which is unusual in itself. (He's been working more regular now that he's trying to impress Sneaky.) He calls us down to breakfast, saying he won some primo sausage last night playing cards with a fellow who works at the locker plant, and he gives it to me to fry up.

He pulls Aunt Glo into the den, but when I hear him tell her that he saw Constance down at the old carnival grounds toting a Mexican baby, I leave the sausage to fry by itself and stand in the doorway to listen.

It's funny, how hope can change a person's disposition. In photographic terms, it's like someone has enhanced Aunt Glo. Her whole face sharpens. She asks, "How'd she seem?"

"Strung out," Tim-Tim says. "Skinny." He shakes his head. "She looks about how Daphne'd look wearing your clothes."

"Is the baby hers?"

"Don't know," Tim-Tim says. "I reckon." He looks around, sees me standing in the doorway, and asks, "Where's Daphne?"

"Bathroom," I say.

"Good," he replies.

"She got anywhere to stay?" Aunt Glo asks. "Where's she staying?"

"Up the road somewhere, at the migrant camp, I'm guessing. I told her to stay her ass away from here."

"She's your sister," Aunt Glo whisper-scolds.

"Momma," Tim-Tim says, and he grabs her by both shoulders and pushes her a little. "Think about Daphne."

Daphne comes trotting in, and I run to flip the sausages and turn on the vent. "Morning, booger," Tim-Tim says.

"Don't call me booger," Daphne says. "Just 'cause you got a girlfriend with a nickname don't mean I need one."

"Oh-ho," Tim-Tim says and grabs her, tickling. "Well, excuse me, Miss Priss."

"Don't you call me Miss Priss!" she says, wiggling around in his arms.

"Honey," Aunt Glo says to Daphne, "run wake up Quin. He's gonna miss the bus."

So Daphne takes off hollering for Quincy to get up.

"I didn't wanna tell you," Tim-Tim says. "But I didn't want you to run into her at the store or anything."

Aunt Glo nods. She's gone over to the refrigerator, where there's still a picture of Constance up. It's the only one in the house, a picture from when Constance was about three or four and Tim-Tim was still in his baby seat.

"She's a whore, Momma," Tim-Tim says.

"Don't act like you so much better," Aunt Glo snaps. "What were you doing at the carnival grounds, anyway? Nobody's up to no good at the carnival grounds."

S O THAT'S THE FIRST THING.

The next thing happens when the school bus passes the old post office where Quincy and Roger and the other boys do their skateboard stunts. There's a demolition crew at work, knocking the whole place down, and a big banner stretched from the light pole to a hickory tree with Dino Honeycutt's logo: COMING SOON: LUXURY CONDOS.

I know that's a bad omen. The town's already raised the water bill so high that Aunt Glo's cousins have all moved out to the country. Last time they reassessed property values, her uncle Ernest sold his house on the next block and moved with his wife to Tennessee, where you can get a double-wide and ten acres for what a house in town is worth. Whenever Aunt Glo gets in one of her moods, the kind where she goes to the grocery store and pushes the buggy all along the aisles without putting any groceries in it, she always winds up talking about what we'll do when they force us out. We'll sell the house and buy some land out of town, she says to the canned goods. Or we'll keep the house but rent it to rich people and move over the county line where the supervisors aren't fools and nobody put bond initiatives on the ballots. She stands in front of the greeting cards and mutters about how rich folks are ruining everything, coming in from other places and buying up property, then spending so much renovating it that regular people can't afford it. They're the reason all our taxes get hiked.

So I see that LUXURY CONDOS sign and know that when I get home, Aunt Glo will be high on whatever's in Irene Earle's prescription bottle. I might be fixing up that workshop for nothing. If Dino Honeycutt brings high-dollar housing to the very next block, we won't be living at 206B Osprey Lane for very long.

THE THIRD THING HAPPENS RIGHT after supper. Aunt Glo shows me an envelope from the prison with Daddy's inmate number written in pencil beneath the return address. Inside, there's a visitation form for the very next weekend. They go in alphabetical order at his prison, and it's Daddy's turn again. But we get these forms every few weeks, and we never go. The car's too old to make the trip, and we don't have the money.

"We're not going, are we?"

"Leaving Friday afternoon," Aunt Glo says. "You can all skip school."

Daphne and Quincy high-five at this news, but not me. I'm thinking about our slick tires, the alternator that keeps going. It's not safe.

"What about the car?" I ask.

"Tim-Tim's borrowing us a van," she says. "Belongs to his boss."

"He must be in good with the boss," I mutter. I wonder what would happen if I put sugar in the gas tank and stalled it, whether Tim-Tim would get fired for that. I don't really want him to get fired, not when he's starting to do better. Lately they've been letting him keep the company truck over the weekend.

"Sneaky's coming, too," Aunt Glo says. "You like her, don't you? The van's got plenty of room."

"I can't go," I tell her and try to look apologetic about it. "I've got a big project at school. And I've got to finish the workshop."

"It's been three years, Kenny," she says. "I can't keep lying to the man."

"I don't want to see him," I tell her.

"You're going," she says.

To keep from thinking about it, I take pictures. Ms. Brady (Saraswati) has loaned me a little silver digital camera with a zoom in/zoom out button. I roam the halls of the Tech Center and snap shots of everything—the horticulture class mixing chemicals for their rootings, the culinary arts students chopping up vegetables with shiny knives. In the main office, I take pictures of the assistants waving to me from the copy machines, from the mailboxes. For every picture I keep, I have to get the names of all the people, so I carry a little black notebook for that purpose.

In automotive repair, the teacher poses with the girls beside the brake fluid, and I capture his grin for all posterity. I take another of him illustrating the proper way to check your lugs. In return, he lets me leave to take more pictures while the rest of the class installs brake pads.

I sit on the bench right outside the main office and scroll through my pictures, deleting the bad ones, and I try not to think about Daddy there at prison. The last time I saw him, he said I looked terrible, and couldn't I spruce up for my old man? I told him I had a cold, but Aunt Glo knew. I'd already stopped trying to look like a girl. I'd stopped caring if he liked how I looked.

The next year I came down with the stomach flu the same weekend she went to visit. Really. I was glad for it, too, and didn't even care that I spent the weekend crashed out on the bathroom floor covered in my own mess, only two steps from the commode but too sick to get to it. I'd be that sick again if it'd keep me away from the prison.

Aunt Glo almost talked me into going the time after that. But at the last minute, I lost my nerve and jumped out of her Ford Escort at a red light and took off through the trees. She looked for me for a little while but finally had to go on or else miss the chance to see Daddy at all. It's not that easy for her to take off on weekends. She hardly ever gets two days off in a row.

I don't fault Aunt Glo for wanting to see him, 'cause they've loved each other a long time, since he was eighteen and in the navy, and she was the older woman who helped him open his account at the credit union. He'd never been in the city in his life and didn't know how to get his phone turned on, didn't remember his zip code to put on his checks. So she looked up his zip code and drew him a map to the phone company and told him the best place to get a drink after work.

When he got there that same night, she was waiting tables. She was married then, but her husband was deployed. She was working two jobs, and her with a two-year-old already. Daddy cheered her up the whole long season, since his ship was getting an overhaul. If fate hadn't stepped in, she and Daddy might have gotten together, but her husband came back, and the family transferred to San Antonio, where Tim-Tim was born.

About that time Daddy met my momma in a waterfront bar where she played acoustic guitar. She'd left home early, severed her ties, and she'd always wanted to be a part of the Atlanta music scene. So she climbed into his little Volkswagen Bug—the old-fashioned kind that stalled when it rained—and took a road trip to Georgia with Daddy. Daddy wasn't the only one good at mechanics. It was Momma who figured out that you could get an extension cord and use a regular blow dryer to dry off the VW engine. They broke down in South Carolina but were back on the highway in no time flat.

There are pictures of her big-pregnant with me and playing in clubs. She sat on a stool and played her guitar sideways, balancing it on the edge of a chair and the tip of one knee.

Daddy showed me the pictures after she died. He kept them on a high shelf in his closet, and we'd take them down sometimes and look at them together. When we moved to Aunt Glo's house, most of our stuff traveled in the back of his pickup truck, but those pictures rode right up front between us in a red-and-white cigar box.

After he went to prison, I kept the box. I looked at the pictures too much, though. I'd take them out in the middle of the night and study them again first thing in the morning. That was back before I had Clara and Rhonda to think about, back before oranges and Irene Earle.

Finally I gave the cigar box to Aunt Glo. She put it some-where, and I haven't gone spying. She'll give it back anytime I ask. That's why I'll have to go with her to see Daddy in prison, if she begs me.

In the pictures Daddy took of Momma, he always put her dead in the center, but according to Ms. Brady (Saraswati), a good photographer knows how to offset an image to emphasize a particular aspect.

I get a few photos of the EMT students resuscitating their dummies, and then I call it a day. Since I still have the camera, I take some shots on the school bus. There are never any bus shots in yearbooks. Maybe I could talk Ms. Brady into putting together an entire yearbook of school bus photos, and I could record the things that go on behind the scenes, the grabbing between the legs when girls walk down the aisles, the boys with their straight pins, the fights, the graffiti, the backseat sex.

I snap a picture of Sudie Montgomery's cheerleading skirt and panty-hosed legs when we get to her stop, her pom-poms dangling from one hand, her other hand dragging her book bag, which isn't zipped all the way. It's one of the kinds with wheels that you pull like a suitcase.

Then I zoom in on a ninth-grade boy with blue acne and braces. He's across the aisle and back a seat, staring out the window and wishing he was dead. But he catches me framing him in my lens, says, "Don't," and holds up his hand.

It's the best picture of the whole day: his hand, his skin (it's so much worse than mine), the dirty bus window behind him with its dirty metal casing. He could be in jail.

"I'll delete it," I tell him, but I don't.

I don't blame Aunt Glo for wanting to see Daddy in prison. They wrote letters back and forth all those years. She told him how she left her husband and moved back to her parents' home. He told her when I was born, sent Momma's obituary through the mail, and Aunt Glo sent flowers, even though they arrived really late. It was a long time before they saw each other again in person.

She talked him into coming for a visit, and we called it a vacation. I'll never forget it, the drive that went on forever, listening to cassette tapes in Daddy's truck, then crossing a bridge so long I thought for sure we'd end up overseas. Tim-Tim and I went swimming in the bay in our Sunday clothes, but Quincy had to play at the edges because he was too little.

The next month we moved right in and made a family, and it worked for a couple of years, until Daddy started coming home drunk and crying on the doormat, snot pouring out of his nose holes like a tiny baby. Then he started taking something that made his mind race all the time, wild and angry, his eyes not even blinking when they should. He went around bragging to everybody about how much his hubcaps cost and was the only one who didn't know what a fool he'd become.

He wound up in jail, then prison, and he's recovered, or so he says. They have A.A. and N.A. at the prison, and he goes to the meetings, and Aunt Glo's proud of him for getting cleaned up, even if he had to be behind bars to do it. But now he and Aunt Glo are stuck writing letters again. So it's no surprise she's hankering to see him in person.

But he ruined my life and left me here a sicko. I'm nothing like the daughter I used to be—but even less like the son he never had. So Aunt Glo has to understand that he's the last person I want to spend my Saturday with.

WHEN I HEAR ON THE EVENING NEWS that a nor'easter's coming, I think maybe we'll skip the trip to the prison. But a nor'easter's no big deal, Aunt Glo claims, and it isn't, not really, not as long as you have enough warning to take down the porch swing so it doesn't bang into the house, and turn the plastic chairs on their sides so they don't blow off and break somebody's window.

"Help me get that flag down, gal," Jarvis Stanley says. "I threw out my back. Can't get it down myself." So while I'm working on our porch, I do his, too. I take down his red-whiteand-blue, roll it up for him around his flagpole, and pass it through his screen door.

"Come on in here and put it in my closet," he says. "I can't get in there with my back acting up."

I think about that horseshoe crab tail and wish I hadn't thrown it to the waves. But Jarvis doesn't do anything except thank me, and I hurry out. He's got a dark slipcover over his couch, and all afternoon I wonder if there's blood splattered beneath it. It doesn't smell that bad in there. Just stale.

I go out to my workshop to secure it as best as I can. It looks nice inside, and since I have Ms. Brady's (Saraswati's) camera there with me, I take a few pictures. I know they don't belong in the yearbook, but I like the idea of having them. I debate bringing the camera along to record our trip, but then remember that you're not allowed to take pictures in prison. Besides that, what if a picture of my daddy wound up in the yearbook by accident? That'd be the worst.

WE'RE SCHEDULED TO BE at the prison at seven-thirty on Saturday morning. If we miss our target time, we'll miss the visit altogether. That's why we have to leave on Friday and get a motel room and spend the night.

There are six of us—Aunt Glo, Tim-Tim, Sneaky, Quincy, Daphne, and me—and it's true that we have a load of room in the van. But Aunt Glo packs a cooler full of fried chicken, cold macaroni, soft drinks, and snacks, so between the food and our suitcases and the taped-up box that Tim-Tim has to deliver for his boss, we have just enough space for six. I was expecting a work van filled with tools and vents and pipes, but this van's nice, maybe the kind that Tim-Tim's boss drives on vacations to

Atlantic City or something. It doesn't even have the logo on the doors like the company trucks Tim-Tim usually drives.

It's late when we get to the motel. Aunt Glo tries to put us all in a double room, but when she asks for two additional roll-away beds, the clerk says no, so we have to get two rooms. Aunt Glo looks like she might cry, but Tim-Tim pulls out a wad of cash and says, "I got it, Momma."

Aunt Glo looks surprised and says, "Where in the world?"

So we get adjoining rooms, a double and a single, three beds in all. Aunt Glo won't let Tim-Tim sleep with Sneaky. He has to sleep with Quincy. Tim-Tim huffs up and starts to say he paid for the rooms, but Aunt Glo gives him a look and he backs down. It wouldn't be right, she says, for *me* to sleep with Quincy, no matter how I dress. I could sleep with Daphne, but then Aunt Glo'd have to sleep with either Sneaky or Quin, and much as she loves him, Quin's too old for that now, and she hardly knows Sneaky at all.

It's a regular puzzle, these sleeping arrangements, and everybody's wishing we'd just gotten two double rooms, so there'd be a bed to spare.

Aunt Glo and Daphne end up in the room to themselves, and me and Sneaky and Tim-Tim and Quincy have the other room. When the door between us closes, Tim-Tim pulls out a joint, and even Quincy smokes a little, but not me. I don't smoke anything. I know the old saying, "Never say never," but I'll say it anyway. Never. Not me.

When Tim-Tim's sure Aunt Glo's out for the night, he and Sneaky take a shower together while me and Quin watch television and try not to laugh ourselves to death at Sneaky squeaking and Tim-Tim grunting the way he does. They tear down the shower curtain. You can hear it crumple and give. And when the water turns off and they open the door, Tim-Tim comes out holding up the handicap rail, which they've torn right off the wall.

We nearly die over that, all of us. Tim-Tim calls the front desk and gets a rollaway bed for Quincy, so he and Sneaky can sleep together, and when the clerk rolls it in, Tim-Tim hands him the handicap rail and says, "It was on the floor when we got here, man. I swear it."

Sometime in the night, Sneaky climbs in bed with me.

She's a real country girl, Sneaky is, with a real country accent. "He's 'bout to kill me with them poots," she tells me, so I slide over, and Sneaky curls right up.

I feel her knees behind my knees. I feel her titties against my back. I lay so still, frigid as the dead, just feeling her there, breathing so tiny against me.

THE NEXT MORNING AUNT GLO gives instructions to Sneaky for taking care of Daphne and Quin. They're both still asleep, and Sneaky's staying with them at the motel while Tim-Tim drops us off at the prison and runs an errand for his boss one town over. He'll be back to collect them before check-out. There are honey buns wrapped in plastic in the cooler for everybody's breakfast.

"Is that what you're wearing?" Aunt Glo asks me.

"Yes, ma'am," I tell her. I've got on a hooded sweatshirt, nothing wrong with that, and I'm wearing it baggy, so even if my tits were free, you wouldn't see them. I've got on my blue jeans and my sneakers, nothing special there, but I leave my ball cap in my suitcase. Aunt Glo works on my hair a little as we drive to the prison. She's brought along some mousse, and she sprays it in my hair and fluffs it up.

"Looking good," Tim-Tim teases.

"Shut up," I tell him. My stomach's a mess, a big knot of hurting.

"How 'bout some lipstick?" Aunt Glo offers. She's pulled out a tube and put some on herself. All I can think about when I see it is a dog prick. Gross.

"No," I tell her.

"Just some ChapStick, then," she says, and I agree. My lips peel most all the time and bleed when I'm not looking.

On the way to the prison, she pulls out earrings—clip-ons that she must have bought for me because her ears have holes. Daphne's ears have holes. My holes have grown over, and I'm glad about it. "No," I say. She pulls out a necklace. Simple. One of Daphne's. A heart on a thin gold chain. No again.

"I'm fine," I hiss, though I'm not. What I really mean is I'm okay the way I am, without jewelry I'll have to take off anyway to pass through the metal detectors. I pretend to look out the window at the brown fields and brown trees, which is all I'd see if I could see through this fog.

We haven't gone a mile when Aunt Glo pulls out the eyeliner and mascara and passes them back like she's offering me a mint. Why can't she leave me alone? I snatch them from her, dammit, and paint it on heavy. I don't even have a mirror, but I don't need one. "Satisfied?" I almost holler. I rim my eyes thick with kohl and blink on the mascara until it's ridiculous. I don't care if it's up to my eyebrows, down to my cheeks.

"Don't be a clown, now," Aunt Glo says.

Tim-Tim doesn't say a thing. He knows better. I'd stab him in the ear with the mascara wand. He just drives us through the first gate, through the tall fence lined with spiral wire, and drops us off at the reception building.

"Be back here by eleven-thirty," Aunt Glo says, and he tells us he will and drives off. Aunt Glo spits on her fingers and wipes at my face like I'm two. I yank away.

After that, it's a whole lot of waiting. I keep my face down so I don't have to look at other families. Don't criminals know that when they go to prison, they sentence their whole families to this shameful shit? And I'm mad at Aunt Glo, so I don't talk. She gives them our application for visitation, with Daddy's inmate number on it, and we wait and wait, like we're seeing a doctor, except longer. Finally they call us up.

Ordinarily, at this point, you put everything in your pockets into a tray—jewelry if you wear it, the quarters you brought for the vending machines—and then you walk through a metal detector. That's what happens for Aunt Glo, but when it's my turn, I'm detained. "No men dressed as women," the officer says, and everybody looks at me. Aunt Glo's way up ahead, but she calls back, "She's not a man. She's a girl!"

"Yeah, right," the corrections officer says, and he's about to frisk me when Aunt Glo comes through the chute. She's near hysterical, saying, "Look at her birth certificate."

Anybody under eighteen has to have a birth certificate along, and sure enough, mine says, Kendra Elaine Lugo.

"Huh," the officer says. He studies me. "No cross-dressing." I think he's about to make me go unbind my titties when Aunt Glo shouts, "Are you trying to give her a complex? Let us through right this minute or I'm calling my lawyer."

We don't have a lawyer. We have a public defender and a guardian ad litem I've never met. But it works.

So we move into another room, where we wait again for the shuttle to take us to Daddy's building, and all the time I'm wondering what it means to be mistaken for a boy trying to pass as a girl rather than the other way around. I don't know which is better or which I prefer, but I'm glad Aunt Glo's with me. I have to sit on the shuttle seat behind her, because there's no room for us to sit together, and I look at her hair frayed out over the seat, the ends burned from her last permanent, and it makes me so sad I want to hug her, but I don't.

The visiting area smells like underarms and bleach, but looks a lot like the cafeteria at school. We sit at a round table with beige plastic chairs and wait another hour for Daddy to come. There are families visiting everywhere, little kids running around, little kids asking their daddies when they're coming home.

There are toys in one section, plastic slides and hideaways for the little kids, and I wish Daphne was with us so I'd have somebody to talk to, somebody to stand beside at the vending machines.

Finally Daddy comes out. He's littler than I remembered, wearing out-of-style aviator glasses, and he has a crew cut, but you can see a lot of his head where there used to be hair. He looks wiry and tired, but he's different from the daddy who visited me under the pier, not half as lost.

"Kendra," he says, and he gives me a hug. He can only hug me for a second or else the guard in the corner will come over and break our visit up. You get two hugs—a hug when you arrive and a hug goodbye. "Look at you," he says, but his voice breaks, and I don't know what he means.

He hugs Aunt Glo. "Glo-baby," he says, and he kisses her, then pulls back and rubs her cheek, and she starts to cry. First thing.

"What is it?" he asks her.

"Nothing," she says. She takes her seat on my side of the table. Except for the hellos and goodbyes, we have to keep the table between us and Daddy. If we break the rules, they might take it out on him after we're gone.

I'm embarrassed, and I worry that Aunt Glo's crying about me and how I look. I worry that she's feeling bad about letting me turn into such a weirdo. I should have put on those earrings, not for Daddy but for her, just this once.

I turn away so they can have some privacy, even though there's no such thing in prison. I shift in my seat and watch a little girl a couple of tables over do her tap-dance routine for her daddy. She doesn't have any music to tell her when to shuffleball-change.

Aunt Glo and Daddy hold hands beneath the table. She tells him about the luxury condos going in. She tells him about Constance and the maybe-Mexican baby. She cries all through this until finally she's doing nothing but hiccupping and apologizing, saying she had to leave her pills in the car because she couldn't bring her pocketbook in.

Daddy tries to cheer her up. He tells her about this mouth

band they have in prison, this bunch of boys who make music with their finger snaps and toe taps, and by filling up their cheeks and tapping them in rhythm.

"Are you in the band?" I ask him.

"'Course I am," he teases. "I do the armpit honks. See?" He pumps out a fart from under his arm, and we all laugh too hard at something that wasn't funny in the first place.

I go over to the vending machines and get some snacks and bring them back. Daddy puts peanuts in his Coca-Cola, like old times, and we pass a MoonPie back and forth. "One of these days, after I get out, we're gonna take a trip, Kenny. Just me and you," he says.

"Really?"

"Yeah," he says. "Where you wanna go?"

"I don't know," I say. I can't even imagine taking a trip with Daddy, not by myself I'm thinking about the Grand Canyon when he says, "I reckon we oughta head south and see what's left of the family. Get you some quality time with your cousins."

"Seriously?" I say, and I must look miserable about it because he laughs outright and says, "Only if you want to, sugar. We can go camping in Pocomoke if you'd like that better."

I try to figure out how old I'll be by the time he's up for parole. I'll be at least twenty-one. Would we share a motel room or a tent if we went off on a trip together?

"You think about it," Daddy says. "Pick us out a place and then call the Chamber of Commerce. They'll send you some brochures in the mail."

In some ways, it seems like the visit lasts forever. In other ways, it's awfully short, and when a bell rings to tell us we have to be back on the shuttle in ten minutes, I'm not ready.

"You all right, pumpkin?" Daddy asks me, and there goes the rest of my makeup, smudging down my face, and tears like I'm trying to compete with the rain I can hear beating at the roof. I hold my face down so my tears will drop onto my jeans. I must have wrapped my titties too tight because I'm getting even less air than usual. I think I might pass out, and then what would happen?

Daddy wants to hug me, but he can't yet, so Aunt Glo does it for him. She holds on to me real good. "You wouldn't believe what Jarvis did," I whisper, because a whisper's all that comes out.

"I heard," he says. "Yant Glo wrote me all about it." He says that—"yant" for "your aunt"—and it makes me so homesick that I cry some more. "Terrible," Daddy says.

"Right next door," I tell him.

"Yant Glo sent me the newspaper clipping. Said you did a real good job helping out that night with the other girl."

"Rhonda," I say.

"Case of mistaken identity," Daddy says. He shakes his head.

"They didn't *look* like criminals," I say, and I feel a little bit bad, being that he's a criminal and everything.

"How a person looks," he starts, and then he trails off, and I can feel my neck prickling hot and heat climbing into my face. "How a person looks don't mean diddly," he says. "Not diddlysquat. You know that, Kenny. You can't judge a person by how he looks."

All around the room, the men look like mechanics, with their blue shirts tucked into their blue pants. But they're not mechanics.

"I know what she means, though," Aunt Glo says. "You think you're safe when you look a certain way."

A certain way. I can't tell if she's talking about the way girls are supposed to look—eyes made up, lips all plump and pink, long hair—or if she's talking about me looking like a boy so I won't be mistaken for a girl. Girls aren't usually shot in the night. They're usually fucked instead.

If you look a certain way, you aren't supposed to get shot in the night. If you look a certain way, you aren't supposed to get fucked. I don't know how to look.

It's so hard to know how to look.

"Someday you might get in a situation like those girls," Daddy says. "Wrong place at the wrong time, you know? It happens."

I can tell he's trying to say something important, so I do my best to look in his eyes, and I manage it for a second or two.

"If that ever happens," Daddy says, "you gotta announce yourself fast. Let 'em know who you are fast." He thinks about this a minute. "The problem wasn't really mistaken identity," he says. "The problem was they didn't let Jarvis know who they *really* were."

The bell rings again, giving us our last warning, and Aunt Glo tries to stuff in all the things she forgot to say. As she's hugging him goodbye, she tells Daddy I'm photographer for the yearbook. She tells him I've learned to lay tiles. Daddy smiles and stares at me, but I'm not sure what his stare means. Then I'm hugging him goodbye, and I feel like I'm drowning, like I'm way down under the waves.

When I come back up, I see that I've left remnants of Aunt Glo's mascara on his blue prison shoulder.

*　　*　　*

We sit in the reception area for a long time after that because Tim-Tim's not back to get us. I use the ladies' room this time along with Aunt Glo. It's not my favorite place but nothing like the bathroom at school, where girls call you "dyke" and stand up on the toilets to look over the stall walls and see if you have a dick and spray hair spray in your eyes on purpose. I wash off the rest of the makeup and try to lay my hair back down, and then I sit quietly in the plastic chairs outside and wait.

Before my daddy got arrested but after he started using drugs, he lost all his good sense and forgot who I was. I knew it was and wasn't his fault, the way he talked about my body, commenting on everything in front of the whole world, Jarvis Stanley included: "I swear, Kenny's grown tits the size of canta-loupes."

He didn't mean to hurt me. When he pinched my butt as I passed by, when he called me onto the porch where he and Jarvis were cracking pecans and drinking whiskey and he told me to kiss him good night, then stuck his tongue in my mouth to make me go "Ugh!" and wiggle away, I don't think he really meant to hurt me.

Maybe he wanted me to know who was in control. Maybe he wanted to prepare me for what girls had coming. But he couldn't have known he was setting me up, that when he was gone and Jarvis was drunk by himself, Jarvis would grab my ass, too, or claim he had a secret—something Aunt Glo wanted him to pass along—then stick his tongue in my ear, hold me tighter when I pulled away, make me sit on his lap before he'd let me go.

Yuncle Jarvis, my daddy called him in those last months, even though he wasn't my uncle. (But neither is Aunt Glo my aunt.) Daddy couldn't have known that Tim-Tim's new favorite food would be cantaloupes, that he'd go around saying,

"I sure got a craving for a cantaloupe," and cut his eyes at me.

BY THE TIME THE VAN pulls back in the parking lot, Aunt Glo's a trembling wreck. She blames her blood sugar, but the first thing she does when she climbs in is fish through her pocketbook for Irene Earle's prescription. She doesn't even notice at first that Sneaky and Quincy and Daphne aren't there—or that Tim-Tim's lip is split and swollen to the size of a little cucumber.

"What the hell?" I say.

"Nothing," Tim-Tim says. "Sorry I'm late."

"What happened?" Aunt Glo asks, and then: "Where's the rest of 'em?"

"Still at the motel, I reckon," he says.

"You reckon?" Aunt Glo looks at the clock and says, "It's way past checkout, Tim-Tim."

"So I'll pay," he says. "Back off In case you can't tell, I'm having a real bad day."

All the way back to the motel, I try to figure out what was in that box he was supposedly delivering for his boss, and why a person expecting a delivery would bust open Tim-Tim's mouth.

Daphne and Quincy are fine, but they've run up the motel bill. They've been playing Super Mario Brothers, which is so out of date but all they had. Sneaky's in a huff until she sees Tim-Tim's face, and then she's over it, calling him "sugar" and dabbing at his sore places with a wet washrag.

We go through a drive-through but eat in the car because Aunt Glo wants to get home and make sure the place didn't wash away. It's still raining, and the road's a mess of standing puddles that pull us sometimes toward the other lane and sometimes toward the ditch. There are cars off the road and whole lanes closed for the wreckers that load them up, but we don't wreck the boss's van. "Thank the good Lord," Aunt Glo says.

When we get into town, Tim-Tim pulls the van right up into the front yard, next to where Aunt Glo parked the Escort—they'd been forecasting all this water. Tim-Tim doesn't want the van to flood out, and the street's already closing in on itself, like a sore throat or a clogged artery, water thick on either side and only a narrow path to drive through.

We hurry in and leave our suitcases in the car for when the rain lets up, so it's not until we're in the house that we hear Jarvis Stanley talking to somebody—a girl who's wailing awful through the wall.

T AKE DAPHNE UPSTAIRS," Aunt Glo tells me. "Now."

"What is it?" Daphne asks.

"Nothing," I say, but I'm still trying to figure it out for myself. At first I think it's Rhonda, but then the crying girl's at the door and Tim-Tim's hollering, "Get outta here. I told you not to come here!"

There's no reason for him to send Rhonda away.

So I nudge Daphne up the stairs, and Sneaky's right behind me.

"What is it?" Daphne asks. "A ghost?"

"No," I say, "go on," because she's stopped partway up. I swat at her bottom, but she turns and wedges herself in the stairwell, clinging to the rail with both hands and pressing her feet against the far wall.

"I ain't going nowhere till you tell me," she says.

"I don't *know*," I say, but I've figured out by then that it's Constance.

"I'm going to see," Daphne replies, and she tries to duck beneath my arm, but Sneaky's there.

Sneaky says, "You promised to show me your Barbies."

We get Daphne moving again, up and into the hall, and I

start singing, which is the dumbest thing in the world to do, but I'm trying to make enough noise to cover up the arguing. "She'll be coming around the mountain when she comes," I sing, and Sneaky gives me the funniest look, but she chimes in, too.

I lock the door behind us and get the Barbie case out of the closet. I bang and clank things around on purpose while Sneaky sings, "We will all have chicken and dumplings when she comes. Yum-yum."

But Daphne's not in the mood for a sing-along. "Cut it *out!*" she shouts. And then she tells Sneaky, "Back before we knew you, Jarvis Stanley killed a girl." Then she turns to me and asks, "Was it the dead girl that screamed or the other one?"

"Other one," I say.

"Everything's all right," Sneaky tells her. "That's just the wind you're hearing."

Daphne looks at me and rolls her eyes. "No, it *ain't.*"

"You stay here with Sneaky," I say. "I'll find out." Sneaky's already taking off the dolls' clothes. Ordinarily Daphne loves to strip them naked, but today she's not interested. "Come right back," she tells me. She grabs my hand and pulls on it to make her point. "Right back!"

ME AND QUINCY PEEK OUT THE WINDOW at Constance and Aunt Glo on the porch. Somebody's beat Constance up, and all she can do is cry and say she's sorry. She leans against the porch post and shakes like a seizure. She shakes so hard that I wish Aunt Glo would hug her, but she doesn't.

The rain's blowing sideways, drenching them both. The roof doesn't help much in this kind of storm. We watch until

Aunt Glo sticks her head in the doorway and hollers for me to bring a lighter, so Constance can light her cigarette.

When I hand the lighter out, Constance keeps her back to me. She hunches over her cigarette, but it's wet and takes a long time to ignite. All the bones in her back stick out, and I can't help thinking about red drum skeletons washing up on the beach, their sharp vertebrae all hooked together.

The wind catches the door, and Aunt Glo pulls hard to shut it. "What are those purple things all over her face?" Quin asks. Constance's skin is a mess of acne and blotches. Tim-Tim, who's laid out on the couch with a bag of frozen peas on his lip, says, "The Hiv."

Quincy says, "What?" and then, "No way."

"She's got The Hiv," Tim-Tim says. "IV drugs. Don't do 'em."

He says "Hiv" like it rhymes with "give." So it takes me a while to figure out they're talking about HIV about AIDS, and we don't know that for sure. There must be other things that cause purple sores on your skin, maybe cancer or maybe not washing.

UPSTAIRS A DOOR SLAMS, and Daphne tries to run back down, but Sneaky grabs her and hollers for me to help. So I go up, and Daphne says, "Don't you try to trick me, Kenny. Just tell me what's going on."

"Nothing," I claim.

"You better not lie to me," Daphne warns. "Did your daddy escape from jail and follow us home?"

"No," I say.

"Are the police here?" she asks.

"No," I tell her.

"Then why can't I come downstairs?"

"It's a bad storm," I say. "You're safer up here with Sneaky."

"I'm scared," she says, and I tell her there's nothing to be scared of. Then I go get her a Christmas present out of Aunt Glo's closet, one Aunt Glo bought early—a little monkey-making kit. It's something Daphne picked out of a catalog a long time back, so she and Sneaky start making sock toys, and I go back down.

AUNT GLO'S JUST INSIDE THE DOOR, dripping on the welcome mat, and Tim-Tim's right in her face, pointing his finger. "She ain't coming in here," he says. "I mean it."

Aunt Glo looks back through the door at Constance, then says quietly, "We both gonna catch pneumonia."

"I don't care," Tim-Tim says. He's blocking the entryway, and I'm surprised at how broad his shoulders look when he pulls himself up like that.

I run to the kitchen to get a dish towel, and Aunt Glo uses it to blot the water from her face. Behind her, Constance steams up the storm door with her breathing. When she wipes the steam away, she spots Quincy and gives him a little wave.

"You don't make the decisions around here," Aunt Glo says to Tim-Tim.

"I do now," Tim-Tim says. "I'm the man of this house, and what I say goes."

Aunt Glo pops him right across the mouth, hard, and I know it must hurt because it's the second time that lip's been bloodied today. Quicker than a blink, Tim-Tim hauls off like he's gonna hit her back.

I cringe, and so does Quin, but Aunt Glo doesn't back down, and in a second or two, Tim-Tim puts his fist in his pocket. He dabs his mouth on his shoulder.

"When *you* pay the taxes," she says. "When *you* pay the car insurance, when *you* start putting the groceries on this table, then you can talk to me about being a man."

Tim-Tim's real even, almost quiet, when he says, "Don't make me stop you, Momma. 'Cause I ain't letting you bring her in this house."

I don't know which one of them to stand by, so I stand by Quincy. I rest my chin on the crown of his head, and he doesn't even pull away.

In the end, Tim-Tim wins. Aunt Glo takes the phone out onto the porch so Constance can call somebody to come get her. But it's gonna be awhile, and it's really not safe outside, not with things blowing like they are, tree limbs and shingles. Aunt Glo bangs on Jarvis's door, but he doesn't come. Maybe he's passed out or maybe he doesn't want to get involved in a family brawl. So we let Constance wait out back in the workshop, because the boyfriend who beat her won't come get her until the rain eases up.

I hate it. I can't even *say* how much I hate it. I want to take the key from under the fern and let Constance hang out at the rental lady's property across the street. But I feel too sorry for Aunt Glo to refuse when she tells me to get the lantern.

Me and Quincy bring out towels and a blanket. You'd think Constance would be glad to have a dry place, but she isn't. "What'd y'all do," she asks, "have a family meeting and decide

I'm too dirty to come in the house?" She's perched up there on top of my cabinets, on that blue float that fell off somebody's yacht. It was going to be my bed one day, but now it's contaminated.

Aunt Glo goes back and forth between trying to explain why Constance can't come in (Daphne shouldn't have to see her own momma that way) and apologizing for it. She even uses that little-girl voice that I hate. She says that Tim-Tim *won't let her* bring Constance in.

"Fuck Tim-Tim," Constance hisses.

Even though Quincy's going on thirteen, he's got ahold of my shirt again, twisting it without knowing. He leans in to me and whispers, "She's a freak."

"She's high," I whisper back—because there's a difference. Being high turns anybody into a freak. No exemptions.

Soon enough, Constance is crying again, apologizing and wondering out loud how her life turned out the way it did. She goes from one emotion to the other so fast, in the time it takes Aunt Glo to run in the house and get her some pretzels. Constance stuffs her mouth as fast as her hands will work.

Then she cheers up a little talking to Quin, asking him if he has a girlfriend yet. When she tells him a story about something dumb he did when he was a baby, she smiles too big, and her teeth are all mustardy-looking—from drugs, I know. I've seen it before.

The wind's raging, so we stay out in the workshop with Constance until she goes off on another rant, this time about how Daphne's *her child,* and if she wants to, she can take her and leave, because nobody has the right to keep her away from *her own child.*

Aunt Glo gets tough then and says if Constance had bothered to show up for any of the custody hearings, she'd know that she'd lost all her rights, and maybe she better spend her energy taking care of the baby the state hasn't already taken away.

But it turns out the maybe-Mexican baby isn't Constance's after all. It belongs to her friend, or so she says. For the baby's sake, I'm glad, but for Daphne's sake, I'm not.

I decide right then that I'm taking a kitchen knife up with me to bed.

I do it, too, later on, after we've gotten Aunt Glo back inside and calmed her down, after we've all dried off. Even though I see the truck lights pull up in the alley, even though I hear the tires spin as the boyfriend almost bogs down, picking up Constance and taking her away, I don't trust her a lick. I've taken the biggest butcher knife we've got.

I CAN'T SLEEP, OF COURSE. Daphne's climbed into the top bunk, and I'm in her bed on the bottom. I've told her we needed to swap beds for the night so I'll be able to get downstairs quick if the water starts coming under the door. It's a mean lie to tell, since it's scared her, but it's not nearly as scary as the truth.

"Will you bail the water out of the house just like you do in a boat?" Daphne asks.

"Sure," I tell her.

"Where will you pour it?"

"Down the sink, I reckon," I say. "Or out the window."

"Will our house wash down the road?" she asks.

"Probably not," I say.

"Do I need to put on my life jacket?" she asks.

"No," I tell her. "You're on the top bunk."

I guess she falls asleep after that because she stops asking questions. The wind blows so hard that the walls shake, the bed shakes, and I can hear something slapping around outside. It seems like forever since we visited Daddy in prison, even though it was only this morning. I've got thoughts of him in my head mixed up with thoughts of Constance, her backbones so sharp and exposed. I've got images of the whole house exploding, boards splintering apart and all of us out in the rain, washing off in different directions.

THE POWER GOES OUT SOMETIME in the night. When I go downstairs, I hold tight to the stair rail because I can't see anything at all. But there's a light in the kitchen, the tiny light from underneath Aunt Glo's microscope, and I'm relieved to see her there, studying her slides. It calms her mind to lose herself in the mystery of science.

Under the microscope, the lowest magnification is where a thing looks most like itself. So if you want to recognize something, you can't go much beyond 4X. At 10X, a thing that looks smooth to the naked eye ends up being hairy. At 40 X, you figure out that a million prickles together turn into something smooth.

We look at Aunt Glo's slide collection together in the night. As the wind blows rain against the windows, hard as a water hose, as the leaning fence cries in the wind, we look at three kinds of bacteria and an onion root—slides Quincy gave her for her last birthday. (He lifted them from the science lab, but Aunt Glo doesn't know it.)

Aunt Glo can't tell which slide she's choosing. She just

feels for them in their blue plastic box, and it's like a surprise. When she puts the slide beneath the stage clips, then we can see what she's picked.

A plant leaf looks like a stone wall along the edges. "Ain't that something," she says. "You'd never know from just looking at it."

A flea leg looks a lot like a horseshoe crab tail. (If we were tiny, we could fight all our battles using flea legs as weapons. I picture me and Constance clicking our flea legs together like swords.)

I concentrate on flea legs so I won't have to think about other things—like all Aunt Glo's disappointments. Not only Constance showing up with The Hiv and disappearing again, but Constance *period*. When Constance was born, Aunt Glo named her after the dormitory she lived in at college: Constance Hall. It shivers my spine to think about that, makes me never want to step foot inside a dormitory as long as I live. I can't stand thinking of Aunt Glo longing for things she'll never have.

So I sit with her and look at a slice of earthworm, human blood, a pine needle.

A green thing isn't really green. It's made up of orange and yellow and blue. There are ears of corn inside the cells of seaweed, and a tiny drop of water looks like a picture of outer space, meteors everywhere, a wet thing dry and dusty as mold.

We look at slides until the night quiets and the rains ease up. Perspective is an amazing thing. We blow things up and scale them down, but none of that has much to do with what they are.

"Do you think she'll come back?" I ask Aunt Glo, and she shrugs like she has no clue.

But everything's transparent if you slice it thin enough.

ALL MORNING TIM-TIM'S CELL PHONE rings. He's upstairs still asleep, but his phone's down here, squashed between the cushions on the couch. It rings over and over, and after a while, Daphne gets up from her video game and answers it.

"What?" she says forcefully. She wants the person on the other end to know what a pest he's been. "No," she says. "If he was here, he'd answer his own damn phone."

"Daphne," Aunt Glo warns.

"He's in the bed with Sneaky," Daphne says to the caller. Then: "No, I'm his little niece." Then: "Hang on."

She picks up a red marker and writes down a phone number on the front of Ms. Brady's (Saraswati's) camera manual, which happens to be sitting on the coffee table. I can't believe it. I hear a holler rising up in my head, but I swallow it. There's always Wite-Out. And I shouldn't have left it there in the first place.

"Okay," Daphne says, and she calls the number back. "Miss Irene," she says. "I'll tell him."

I've taken over Daphne's video game. It's an easy one, where pieces of fruit drop from the sky in batches of four, and you have to line up four bananas or four cherries or four watermelons to eliminate them before they stack too high.

"Turn it! Get the cherries," Aunt Glo directs, but I know

she's just trying to get us all focused on this dumb game and not the phone call.

"Do you know her?" I ask. I bleep out a double, watermelons and cherries both.

"Who?" she asks.

"Irene Earle."

"No," Aunt Glo says. "Watch those bananas," and then we do the pretending we always do, with her acting like I don't know about the pills and me acting the same. Soon enough I've lost the game, and Daphne's saying, "Level Four? You only made it to Level Four? Let me try!" and everything's normal again.

TIM-TIM NEEDS TO RETURN the van to his boss, and since it sits high enough off the ground that the tailpipe doesn't take on water, we go cruising around town before we take it back. The water's receding now that the rains have stopped. But up closer to the bay, where the water's higher, people with kayaks paddle around the streets. We drive right through the water, spraying kayakers and laughing. Everything smells like gasoline, probably from the cars that stalled. Tim-Tim stops so Quincy can wade out and get the tire-stem caps off a choked-out BMW. He's never had the opportunity to steal BMW tire-stem caps before.

You can see the swirls of color in the water from the gas,

and I have a feeling you could light it and watch it burn. So I hope Sneaky doesn't throw her cigarette out the window. We could all go up in ashes if the water caught.

Tim-Tim makes Quincy take off his pants and wring them out before he gets back in the van, and everybody laughs at Quin shivering there in his drawers, complaining about his shriveled-up nuts. We fly his pants out the window while we drive around.

Farther from the bay where the streets are mostly dry, the sewage system has backed up, and little waterspouts shoot from all the manhole covers.

We ride around in circles all over town, taking in the sights. When there's too much water in the roads, we take the alleys. They're always higher. We can't get too close to the pier where the flooding's bad, but I can still see how the wind has pushed back the shingles on the gazebo roof. They stand up stiff like fancy-boy hair.

The water's still real choppy. At the harbor, where the elevation's higher, we park and look out at the bay awhile. It looks like meringue to me, all the whips on top of a pie. But Daphne sees pointy white nipples in those waves.

(I hope she doesn't remember one day. I hope she doesn't wake up one day and hate me.)

Finally, after we drive out to the highway to get ice-cream sundaes, and then after we eat them and go by the gas station to vacuum out the van that Tim-Tim borrowed, we drive back into town and pull into the driveway of a house I've seen a thousand times but never really noticed.

"End of the line," Tim-Tim says. "Pile out."

"What?" Daphne complains. "You expect us to walk from here?"

"Ain't but eight or ten blocks," Tim-Tim says. He rings the doorbell, and a little old woman comes to the door. I try to remember if we've been here before, trick-or-treating. I'm pretty sure we have been.

"Hey, Miss Irene," Tim-Tim says.

She has to be eighty years old. She's stooped over and wearing a hairnet and big plastic glasses. "How'd it go?" she asks him, her voice scratching raspy.

"All right," he tells her. "I got that box delivered."

"Good," she says. "I knew I could count on you, Timmy. You're a good feller."

"I reckon that's all," Tim-Tim says. He nods toward the van. "I filled it up with gas."

Miss Irene hands Tim-Tim some folded-up money and a little brown bag that he rolls up and puts in his pocket. "Thank you, ma'am," he says.

"If you want a little something extra next month, gimme a holler," she says and winks. It's weird to see such an old woman wink.

Tim-Tim looks off sideways, shakes his head. "I don't think I'll be able to," he replies, almost like an apology. "I got a girl," he says, like that explains it, and he motions for Sneaky. She joins him, and he introduces her to Miss Irene.

He doesn't introduce any of the rest of us, that's for sure. We watch from the sidewalk, and Quincy mutters, "Completely pussy-whipped," and I elbow him because he shouldn't talk that way in front of Daphne.

But Daphne doesn't hear. She's splashing in mud puddles. "Mud padeedles," she calls them.

From the way Tim-Tim talks to Irene Earle, real polite

and careful, I realize he's nervous. He must have wanted us all to come with him so he wouldn't be with her by himself. Why else would he have taken us riding, bought us all ice creams?

"All right, then," Miss Irene says, and she shuts the door.

We have a long walk back, and I want to ask Tim-Tim for an explanation, but Daphne's there.

"I thought it was your boss's van," I say.

"It was," Tim-Tim replies. "I was doing a little job for Miss Irene."

"What was in that box?" Quincy asks, but Tim-Tim shakes his head and smiles. "Come on," Quin begs. "You gotta tell us."

Tim-Tim breaks down. "Oh, all right," he pretends. "She crochets blankets. I just delivered her blankets to a fellow out there near the prison who sells them."

"Baloney," Daphne says.

"Oh, you think so?" Tim-Tim teases. He picks Daphne up, throws her over his shoulder, and walks like that, hanging on to her ankles. Daphne laughs and punches at his butt.

When we get to the cross street where Roger lives, Quincy takes off. Then we pass Sneaky's, and she says, "Momma's making a cobbler. Let's go see if it's done."

"We'll catch y'all later," Tim-Tim tells me and Daphne.

I nose toward his pocket, where he's got the brown bag rolled up and tucked away. "You want me to take 'em to her?" I ask.

He raises his eyebrows. "Huh?"

"To Aunt Glo," I say.

"All right," he agrees, and he gives me the brown bag. I put it in my own pocket without even opening it up to look. I didn't know drug dealers could be old ladies, but there's something kind of reassuring about it. I'm glad to know Tim-Tim didn't steal her purse.

Daphne complains about the long walk until I let her ride piggyback. Toward home, the water gets deeper, and soon it's sloshing over my ankles. By the time we're at the old post office, where the wind has shredded Dino Honeycutt's banner, you can't tell whether you're walking on the sidewalk or on the street. One false move and you're wet to your knees. One bad step and you've stomped somebody's dried-up fern, washed off the doorstep and into the road.

I F I'D KNOWN AUNT GLO would have a conniption when she woke up and found us all gone, I'd have left her a note. She was sleeping when we left with Tim-Tim, totally zonked. And we're not in the habit around here of reporting our every move to each other.

"You *walked* back from Irene's?" she says. (It sure sounds like she knows her.) "Tim-Tim let you do that?"

I cut my eyes at her. "Yeah," I say. "What's the big deal?" I get a pot and fill it with some water. "You want a hot dog, Daphne?"

"Yeah," Daphne calls from the den, where she's parked in front of the TV

"What's the big deal?" Aunt Glo repeats, like I'm a total goober.

"How many?" I holler.

"Just one," Daphne says. "Long as we got some tater chips."

Aunt Glo paces between the table and the counter, trying to work out whatever craziness she's got going on. I throw three weenies in the pot and ask her if she wants one. She shakes her head and rubs at her temples, and I wonder if she's hearing voices. Maybe she's full-fledged crazy and needs Irene Earle's pills to hold off hallucinations.

So I give them to her. I root around in my pocket for the tiny paper bag. (When I was little, I got candy in bags that size, little candy-bead necklaces I'd nibble away piece by piece.) I pull out Irene Earle's prescription. "Here," I say and toss it to Aunt Glo. I throw it kind of hard.

She misses, and the bag thuds on the linoleum. Aunt Glo is quick in picking it up. She comes to my pot, where the water's starting to boil.

"Where'd you get 'em?" she asks.

"Where do you think?" I sass, and she slaps me, just that fast. She hasn't done that in a long time. She must be in a slapping mood.

I keep right on cooking my hot dogs, even though the weenies have split. I roll them around with a fork while the singe leaves my cheek. It's amazing, really, how little I care that she's slapped me.

"Maybe you better take one now," I say, "don't look like you can get by very long without 'em," and Aunt Glo hits me again.

I open the cabinet. I take out the bread, three slices. I say, "Daphne, you want mustard?"

"Just ketchup," she says from the other room.

Aunt Glo doesn't seem to know what to do with her hands.

She holds the brown pill bottle with Irene Earle's name on it and thumbs at the cap. It's childproof. It's got a label on it saying not to drink or operate machinery.

"Do you wanna lose her?" Aunt Glo asks, and at first I don't know what she means. "Don't you know that Constance could just *take* her? Just grab her and put her in a car?"

And then don't I feel like a shit?

"I'm sorry," I say, and I am. Aunt Glo's sobbing now, tearing at her hair like it's full of biting flies. "I'm sorry," I tell her, and I fix her a hot dog. I pull her out a chair, and she sits. I get her some Coca-Cola, and the tiny bubbles hiss and break around the ice cubes. "I'm sorry," I tell her, "but you gotta quit this." Her pills are on the table, and I pick them up. When I shake them, they rattle too loud to be such little pills in such a little bottle. I think about pouring them out in the sink and running the water for a long time, letting them dissolve into the pipes with Clara Tinsley's blood.

But I can't do that to Aunt Glo.

I don't know how I get from that place—standing by the table holding her pills—to kneeling on the floor with my head in her lap. "Please," I beg her. "Please, please, please," and Aunt Glo's rubbing my head, and her hot tears drop on the back of my neck.

I look up and she's nodding.

I wear her desperation like a collar.

I LOCK THE DOOR BEHIND ME SO Aunt Glo will feel safe. We've all got keys, so it's no big deal. I take a bucket and some bleach out to the workshop, thinking I'll scrub down the cabinets and the blue float. Cleaning always calms me down, and maybe Constance will never come back. Maybe she'll disappear like a red Pontiac. I picture her driving off in one, right off the face of the earth.

I want to hate Constance. In some ways, I hate her. But without her, I wouldn't have Daphne.

Daphne was Constance's first big mistake, a mistake so big she didn't even stay around to raise it. But Daphne's my favorite person on the planet, even if I want to stick her head in the commode sometimes.

So I can't *just* hate Constance. In fact, the whole time I'm cleaning, I'm sort of appreciating her.

Because sometimes you need someone like Constance to remind you of how bad things could be. I don't have The Hiv, and I'm not a drug addict. I might be a sicko with a lifestyle and not even a high school diploma, but I'm not all cracked up.

My hatred seeps back in, though, when I go to look for the camera.

It isn't in my backpack—and then I remember that I emptied my books so I could use my backpack as a suitcase on our prison trip. And then I remember that I took pictures of the workshop right before we left. So I must have left it there.

It's gone, of course. Constance stole it. Ms. Brady's (Saraswati's) camera.

THERE'S NOTHING FOR ME TO DO except pace the beach. Low tide looks like high tide now, but the beach is a whole new place, all our old footprints washed away, the remnants of Clara Tinsley's shrine washed away, Rhonda's long gone. I make new footprints up and down the shoreline. The heels of my sneakers press a pattern that looks like hooves, and I try not to step down on my toes too heavy, so anybody who comes after will think a deer's been pacing instead of just me.

If I was a deer, I'd run off. But where?

If I was a deer, maybe somebody'd shoot me and gut me and stew me into hash.

I wish a little bit to be dead and gone myself because sometimes I get tired of how every day brings a new problem. It seems like it never ends. And I don't think that happens just to me, either. It happens to everybody, probably even Wendy Honeycutt.

I've used all my savings fixing up the workshop. I don't have ten dollars to my name, and most of what I've got's in change. Cameras like the one Ms. Brady had—I don't even know how much they cost. A lot.

Up in the dunes and pushed into the pathways where you walk onto the beach, there's an outline of sea straw, driftwood, things that didn't survive the storm, a seagull washed up and partly covered by grasses and trash. When the tide pulled back, the storm marked its name. A few dead birds, a few dead fish, and a living dog checking out the damage and peeing on everything that died.

I can't face her, Ms. Brady. She's been so nice to me. She's the only one at school who puts her hand on my back when she passes, or offers me M&M's sometimes if she's got a pack. So I know I can't go back to school, not until I've replaced the camera. I try to remember what kind it was as I walk up and down the beach.

I MAKE POSTERS AND TACK THEM to the light poles, offering to do odd jobs. NO JOB TOO SMALL, I write, hoping to get people like Miss Mattie down the road to let me rake her leaves or do something she might otherwise do herself.

I earn ten dollars right off the bat, helping the Baptist preacher rehang a downspout at the church. But when I dig the newspaper out of the trash to scavenge the sales flyers, I see that a digital camera, even a cheap one, will take awhile to pay for.

I'm limited in when I can work, because my first obligation is to look after Daphne when Aunt Glo's not home. All day Sunday, I think about that camera manual with Irene Earle's phone number on it and wonder whether she'd give me a job if I called her. It makes my heart race to think about it. I picture myself at the old carnival grounds, crouched behind the Ferris wheel with my pockets full of little brown bags of pills. Every time I dial Irene's number, I hang up before it rings.

If Aunt Glo knew I was skipping school, she'd blister me, so I pretend. On Monday morning, after Aunt Glo drives Daphne to school (so she can talk to the teachers and principal about Daphne's safety), I convince Quincy that I'm catching a ride with Wendy Honeycutt. After he gets on the bus, I take my backpack and walk up to Irene Earle's house.

It's a long walk. Every step I take, I know the minute I offer her my services, I'm risking prison. I picture my daddy, and it's a sad thought, knowing I could wind up in the same shape, and me not even addicted. Somehow that makes it worse.

But if I can make a hundred dollars in a single day—or maybe more—then it's worth the gamble just this once. There ought to be some kind of penalty, right? Some kind of risk, since I lost Ms. Brady's camera?

When I get there, Irene Earle's outside. She's wearing a housedress and a butter-colored sweater, her back hunched over so far she looks like a sickle. She's got her broom out, and she's sweeping off her sidewalk.

"Morning, ma'am," I say, and she stops sweeping, leans on her broom, and stares at me.

"I was wondering," I say—but it makes me nervous, how she looks at me—"I was wondering if you had any work you needed done."

"Work?" she asks, and I nod. "What kinda work?" It's a loaded question. One I don't know how to answer. She pulls a pack of cigarettes out of her pocket, shakes one out, and lights up.

I've turned red, I know, but I keep talking. "Anything, really," I say. "Whatever you need." I don't mention drugs, of course, and she doesn't say anything at all. The cigarette droops out of her mouth, and since I can't look at her eyes, I look at the ash, how it grows. She doesn't flick her ashes away. "I could detail your van," I offer and point to it there in the drive.

Beyond it, there's an old boat, barnacles glued to the bottom. Nobody likes scraping off barnacles, so I step over toward the boat and say, "I could clean this up for you." I've chiseled off barnacles before.

What I don't see is the dog tied to the trailer. He's been laying down under the boat, and he jumps out at me, all teeth and froth. Seems like he comes from nowhere, and I run back, leaping out of his reach just in time.

Irene Earle doesn't apologize. She doesn't even try to quiet down the dog. She just says, "Who sent you here?"

I can't tell if Tim-Tim would be a good reference or not. I don't want to get him in trouble. I don't want to step on his turf, either, if he *has* some turf So I say, "Nobody," and take a good look around in case there are other dogs ready to jump out at me from other directions.

She scowls at me. "Nobody who?"

"Never mind," I say, and I back away from her, from the snarling dog still testing its chain. I back down the just swept sidewalk. "Sorry to bother you," I add.

"Don't come back around here," she says. She holds up her broom like she might thwack me with it if she was close enough. "I don't like how you look."

So I go, but it hurts my feelings. It's crazy, I know, because she's an old drug dealer, so why do I care if she likes me? But I try to be nice to *everybody,* drug dealers included, and what's the matter with the way I look? Maybe she thinks I'm with the police.

IF I WASN'T DESPERATE, I'd go to the beach and lay down in the sunshine, but I need money. The only other person who's shown any interest in hiring me is Jarvis Stanley, and doesn't that just figure? He keeps leaning out his door and saying, "Come on over here, gal. I need to talk to you," but I'm putting that off as long as I can.

So I take a deep breath and creep over to Dino Honeycutt's job site, where I muster up my courage and ask to speak to the boss.

Most of his crew doesn't speak English, and I didn't take Spanish for my language. I took French for one semester, and when you go to the Tech Center, you don't have to study languages anymore. Somehow the message gets through, though, and in a little bit, Dino drives up in his truck.

I offer him my hand right away and shake as firm as I can. "Do you have any work for me, sir?" I ask him. He looks at me funny, like he thinks he knows me, or he used to, and he says, "Why aren't you in school?"

I say it before I even mean it: "I had to quit."

"That's too bad," he says.

"I'm studying for my GED on weekends," I tell him, even though I don't have a clue what's on the GED. Somewhere there's a study guide, though. Tim-Tim had one. I try to remember where I saw it. Under the TV stand with all the warranties and directions?

Dino motions me to his truck, and I get a little scared. But I tell myself he's Wendy's daddy, and she's probably ridden in this same truck a thousand miles. It smells like WD-40 in there.

He takes me to a job site way out of town where two boys, Juan and Fredo, are putting in fence posts. It looks like they're fencing in the whole county.

So all week I work for Dino Honeycutt. The first day I'm nervous around the guys, but they don't bother me. They pull out their measuring tapes and measure and smile. They stick their measuring tape into the hole I've dug to see if it's two feet deep. They heave the posts into the holes, and check with their levels, and measure again, and point to where the next hole goes.

I alternate between the shovel and the posthole digger, starting with the shovel but switching over when the hole's too deep. My hands cramp from stabbing the digger into the ground, and my shoulders ache from pulling it up. Sometimes we switch off, and I do the measuring, or pour bags of concrete into the holes around the posts, or lug over buckets of water to mix it all up. Sometimes when Fredo and Juan start laughing, I worry they're laughing at me. But I'm taller than them both and always within hand's reach of a weapon.

Dino Honeycutt himself brings us lunch, hamburgers and drinks from the store where Aunt Glo works, and it doesn't even matter that I don't like mayonnaise. I eat it all the same.

Dino Honeycutt pays me thirty dollars a day, cash, a crispy twenty and a crispy ten. He'd pay me forty, but I can't work past three. He comes to pick me up and drops me off at Aunt Glo's while Juan and Fredo are still working, because I have to be there in time to meet Daphne's bus, and I always need a shower.

I DON'T TELL AUNT GLO about the camera. There's nothing she can do. It's not like she has the money to buy me one. But I let it slip to Tim-Tim, thinking maybe he'll get me in on a game of quarters. Now that Dino Honeycutt's demolished the old post office, I'm not sure where the older boys are playing, but it'd be worth the risk if I limited myself to twenty dollars and turned it into forty—or even more.

Sometimes I practice in my dreams, flicking quarters with my thumb, trying to get mine to shoot up to the bricks and then drop there without rolling back.

"Damn, Kenny," Tim-Tim says and sneers like I'm lower than a possum. "I quit rolling quarters when I was fourteen." That's a lie, and he knows it. But he's a big man now, playing cards, and I probably couldn't win at cards.

He bets on things I don't understand.

Later in the week, though, he comes to me with a business proposition. In the company truck, he drives all the way out to Dino Honeycutt's never-ending fence to talk it over. I don't know it's him at first, until he steps out and sticks his fingers in his mouth and gives a sharp whistle.

I put down my shovel and jog over. I'm glad to take five. We're digging holes through pampas grass roots. You can hardly break them.

Tim-Tim wants me to have sex with Sneaky. She's always wanted to try it with a girl, he says. She's curious, and it'd be easier for her with somebody who looks like a boy.

"You're kidding," I say.

"Fifty dollars," he tells me.

"No way," I say.

"How come?" he asks. "That's good money. It's not like you're a virgin or anything."

I can't believe he'd say it without the first bit of guilt. That's the problem with men—they have the hardest time understanding when they've done something wrong.

"I know you like Sneaky," he teases. "And she likes you."

But she's like my sister-in-law or something, almost—

"You got a rubber dick?" Tim-Tim asks.

"What?" I say. "God!" The flush in my face is instant, scalding. I look to see if Juan and Fredo are listening, but that's silly. Even if they know some English, they wouldn't be able to translate *that*, and besides, they're too far away. "No!" I say. How could Tim-Tim think such a thing?

"Well, you better get one. How you gonna fuck her?"

I picture Quincy and Daphne wiggling their index fingers: "I know, I know."

"I'm *not* gonna fuck her," I say.

"Don't you like her?" Tim-Tim asks. "I'm gonna tell her you think she's ugly."

"I *don't* think she's ugly," I say. "Don't tell her that. She's really pretty."

"I knew it," Tim-Tim says. "She turns you on."

No matter what I say, it goes wrong.

Tim-Tim asks, "You wanna just go down on each other?" He's serious. "She could probably get into that."

"No way," I say. "I gotta go." And I do, because what if Dino Honeycutt shows up? Fredo and Juan have almost finished a hole since Tim-Tim and I started talking.

"All right," Tim-Tim says. "But think about it."

Now I know why somebody might have popped him in the mouth when he went to deliver Irene Earle's blankets, or pills, or whatever he was delivering. Tim-Tim has more nerve than anybody should. It's a wonder he doesn't get a bloody lip every day of his life.

But it's nothing to him, nothing. So is there something wrong with me? If it doesn't mean anything to Tim-Tim and it doesn't mean anything to Sneaky, if they both think it'd be fun, and if they'd pay me fifty dollars, then what's the matter with me? The pampas roots are so tough I can hardly break them. I jump on the shovel with both feet and only sink it an inch.

I make everything into a big deal. Other people just let things slide. Me, I've got to turn them into soap operas. Juan and Fredo shrug and dig, whistle and wiggle their posts around. Nothing seems too hard for them.

I jump and jump, breaking through the roots one layer at a time. I sweat and worry. I fight that shovel, finally prying into the softer dirt where fat earthworms burrow.

To me, everything feels like work.

THAT FRIDAY AFTERNOON, early—definitely before quitting time—Wendy's black Camaro drives down the road and slows. My heart sinks as soon as I see it, and drops to my belly when the car pulls off the side. I hope like crazy that Dino's borrowed her car, maybe taken it in for servicing, but it's Wendy, all right. And I'm filthy nasty, with dirt caked to the knees of my jeans and packed into the wedges of my sneakers. I don't want her to see me like this.

"Kenny," she calls. "Come on."

"What?" I shout.

"Daddy sent me to get you," she says.

So I wave goodbye to Fredo and Juan, and I'm blushing before I even jump the ditch. I don't want to leave clods in her nice car.

"It's okay," she says. "Really. Don't worry about it."

So I knock the dirt off my shoes as best I can, brush off my knees, and get in. The seat feels so low to the ground.

Wendy cranks the car, but we sit there. She doesn't pull away. She tells me she had a dental appointment and had to leave school early, and after that, she met her daddy at the jewelry store to help him pick out some earrings for her momma's birthday.

"You fooled him," she says. "He didn't know who you were. He figured it out when we were at the soda fountain getting a drink and I told him you'd missed school all week."

"You told your daddy about me?"

"Sure," she says. "I've been worried about you. I thought you were sick."

I think, *I* am *sick. A sicko with a lifestyle.*

"But your daddy doesn't know me," I say.

"You came to my birthday party," she reminds me. "Twice. You don't look the same, exactly, but in a way, you do."

"Oh," I say.

"He wouldn't have ever brought you out here if he'd known," Wendy apologizes. She puts the car in gear and pulls off, and I wonder if I'm getting fired, and if I'll get paid my money for today.

According to the clock on her car radio, it's 2:28 P.M., so of course I assume that she's taking me home. But she heads to the high school instead.

"No," I tell her. "I can't go back."

"You have to," she says. "You're smart, Kenny. This is crazy. You can't just quit."

"Please," I say.

"You could go to college. You could get a scholarship."

My throat's getting thick, folding in on my words, so I don't say any more.

"We'll go talk to the principal," she says. "I'll go with you."

"Look at me," I say. I'm filthy.

"It doesn't matter," she says.

But it matters. I smell bad. I can smell my own self I don't want to see any of the kids in my classes. It's bad enough seeing Wendy. And I do that thing I hate. I crumple up my face. "I lost Ms. Brady's camera," I admit. "Saraswati's."

"Don't call her that," Wendy scolds.

"I was supposed to take pictures for yearbook," I tell her. "And somebody stole it."

"Who?" she asks.

"I don't know," I tell her. "But it's gone." I dab at my nose with my dirty fingers, and if my face wasn't smudged before, it is now. I can't go to school looking like this. "I have to replace it," I say. "Or give her money for it or something."

I feel like I'm gonna blow apart. Everything was going fine. I was doing fine. I was making thirty dollars a day, and that adds up.

Wendy parks in the visitor space in front of the school. "Let's go talk to Ms. Brady," she consoles, but I can't do that. Ms. Brady's called the house two times this week to check on me, thinking I'm sick, and I've deleted her messages (to keep

Aunt Glo from finding out) and ignored them without the first explanation. Ms. Brady deserves better.

"She'll understand," Wendy says. "They probably have insurance on the camera."

I hadn't even thought of that, but I say, "Please take me home." When she doesn't make any effort to move the car, I say, "Wendy, please. I gotta be there for Daphne, or something might happen."

Wendy sighs, backs the car out of the space, and heads for Osprey Lane.

I'M ALL CLEANED UP BY THE TIME Dino Honeycutt arrives.

"Hello, sir," I say. I know I should invite him in, but I don't, because Aunt Glo has given strict orders that we're not allowed to have strangers inside, and what would Daphne think?

"Kenny," he says, and shakes my hand. Then he pulls out his wallet and gives me a twenty and a ten.

I pass the ten back. "I knocked off early," I say.

He doesn't accept it. "I want you back in school next week," he says.

"But—"

"I've taken care of this thing with the camera," he says. "Wrote a check to your teacher for the full amount. It's paid for."

How can that be? How can something so hard for me be

so easy for him?

"I can't let you do that, sir," I say, and he smiles pitiful at me. He's trying to be compassionate, I know, maybe even a father figure. He's doing this for me because he loves Wendy, but what he doesn't understand is that replacing the camera doesn't fix my problem.

"It's just a tax break, Kenny," he says. "When you're older, I guarantee you you'll understand. I *make* money when I donate a camera to the school."

I don't know if that's the truth or not. Maybe if you're as rich as Dino Honeycutt, it is.

"I played football with your principal," he says. "I'm gonna give him a call tonight, get things right for you to go back to school."

"You don't have to do that, sir," I say. The truth is, I like not being in school, nobody hassling me, picking on me. I like working with Juan and Fredo. If it doesn't work out for me to be an armored car delivery guard, I can start a fencing company: picket fences, privacy fences, whatever.

"You finish school," Dino says. "And if you want to come work for me then, I'll hire you back."

W ITH THE CAMERA PAID FOR, there's no reason for me to have sex with Sneaky, but I keep thinking about it anyway, wondering what it would be like.

I get some tangerines—they're looser than oranges—and practice taking the sections apart with my tongue. I wonder what Sneaky would taste like. Not citrus, but what?

I try not to think about sex, but sometimes it happens in spite of me. I get that warm camphor burning between my legs. I try to stop it with mind power, to distract myself by reciting the noble gases from the Periodic Table—I had to learn those in ninth grade: helium, neon, argon, krypton, xenon, radon. But that doesn't work. I wonder if the noble gases will be on the GED. I squeeze my thighs together until the feeling passes.

Sneaky's a real sweet girl, little, and I can't stand to think about Tim-Tim pounding into her. I know how he roots, how, when he gets started, you can't stop him to save your life, and it doesn't even matter if his sharp hip bones are bruising the insides of your thighs. It seems like there should be a nicer way to love than that. I suspect there's a nicer way, but I wonder if Sneaky does.

I know it's wrong to think of Sneaky, but when I'm thinking about her, I'm not thinking of Clara Tinsley. I'm not thinking about Rhonda and how she smelled that night on our couch. When I'm thinking about Sneaky, all my dread goes away, and I feel something else, something I can't name.

People already think I have a questionable lifestyle, so what difference does it make? I take the egg whisker out of the kitchen drawer and sneak it up to the bedroom, and I close the soft wires tight with my hand and wrap masking tape around it over and over. The bottom end's too skinny, so I wrap a tube sock around it and tape that up, too, and then I have something like a rubber dick, but not really. It's not flexible, so I get rid of the egg whisker altogether and just use the tube sock and tape, a whole roll of it.

I don't have anywhere I plan to stick it, but I put it in my underpants all the same and walk around, feeling it for a while. If I had one for real, I wouldn't want a big one, not the kind that peeps out the leg of your gym shorts or anything. Just a little one would be fine.

I eat a plum with that sock in my underwear, and it drives me crazy, how slippery a plum is.

If I had one for real, I bet I'd play with it all the time like other boys do. I wonder what it feels like to have a real one, attached. I wonder if other boys position it beneath them so when they lay on their bellies and rub, it shoots shudders all through them.

M Y FIRST DAY BACK IN ENGLISH CLASS, I don't get a chance to talk to Ms. Brady. Other students beat me to the room, so I just take my seat. When she calls the roll, I say "here" without raising my eyes. We have a quiz on a book I haven't read, so I guess at the true/falses and leave the rest blank. I write across the bottom: "I'm very sorry about your camera, ma'am."

It doesn't seem right for me to go to the yearbook work-room at lunch, not after I lost the camera, so I go to the cafeteria, and I circle around slow, but there aren't enough seats, and you can't just plop down anywhere. The band students all sit together and put their music cases on empty chairs. The cheerleaders cluster with the soccer team. Even the misfits have their cliques, and I'm not invited. I circle the perimeter. Somebody throws a piece of tomato on my sneaker, but I don't look to see who. I wish Wendy had first lunch, but she has second. A kid from Morning Devotional pretends not to see me.

So I find a corner and back into it. I pull out my keyboarding workbook and act like I'm reading it while I eat my banana first and then my apple.

That's where Ms. Brady finds me.

"Kenny," she says. "Can I see you?"

A piece of apple skin hangs in my throat. "Sure," I say, and I gather up my things and follow her back to her room. My heart's throbbing, oh, it's pounding me so hard, and my mouth's so dry in spite of my apple, and even though I'm trying not to cry, I can feel the tears rallying behind my eyes. As soon as she closes the workroom door, they break through.

Ms. Brady's real even about it all, though. "Whatever happened," she says, "I know it wasn't on purpose."

"It wasn't," I say. I'm talking into the blackboard, my cheek washing the blackboard, because I can't bear to turn around.

"Kenny, when something goes wrong," she says, "I want you to be able to talk to me."

"I'm sorry, ma'am," I say again.

She puts her hand on my back and keeps it there, and it seems like a long time before I can make the shaking inside me stop. But when I quiet down, she turns away. Her shoes clop across the room, over to the file cabinet.

"We have a deadline," she says. "I need those pictures from the Tech Center."

"They're gone," I tell her. I don't look up at her because I know how ugly I am when I cry—believe me, I know. Some people get cute, Daphne, for example, but not me. I puff up red, and my eyes get all piggy. "I didn't download them," I say.

"You'll have to retake them." She unlocks the file cabinet and pulls out a brand-new camera, different from the one Constance stole, this one still in its box.

"You're kidding."

"No," she says. "You're my only correspondent out there. I can give you until the end of next week."

"But what if it gets stolen again?" I whisper. I hardly have any air left inside me. Ms. Brady says, "It won't."

THAT WEEKEND WHEN THE RENTAL LADY comes to check on her property, she brings an old woman who turns out to be her mother. It's cold out, but the mother sits on the porch with her feet in the sunshine and smiles at the sky so sweetly it's hard to believe her daughter could ever be involved in a wrongful-death civil suit. I think, *That lady's like me*—one step removed from a criminal past—and I wonder what it did to her to see her daughter's picture in the newspaper, to hear her daughter's name on the evening news.

I take the mother's picture with the new camera, just for practice. Ms. Brady said it was fine for me to practice, and next week we'll burn my pictures to a disk, and then one day when I have a computer of my own, I can look at them and remember.

If the rental lady goes to prison, I wonder who'll take her mother to visit. She seems too old for prison visits.

It's hard to picture the rental lady having a mother at all. This old lady goes for a walk down our street, but the side-walks are all bumpy, with tree roots breaking back through the concrete. Somehow she trips and falls—Quincy tells me about it later. And it's Jarvis Stanley, of all people, who goes to help her up. He gives her his arm and walks her back to her porch.

O VER AND OVER, AUNT GLO CHECKS the locks. She even gets a free estimate for a security system we'll never be able to afford. But we don't see any more signs of Constance.

Then Miss Mattie from down the street comes by and tells Aunt Glo that when she was on the way to the monthly widow luncheon yesterday, she saw Constance hitchhiking, thumb pointed south. Miss Mattie couldn't let her do that, not knowing how dangerous truckers can be, so she picked her up and drove her to the bus station.

"Oh, thank you, Lord," Aunt Glo says.

Constance only had enough money to get to Savannah, but

she was trying to get to Miami, where she said she had a friend. So Miss Mattie loaned her thirty dollars to make up the difference, plus a ten to get her a hamburger or two.

Aunt Glo goes through her wallet, looking in all the compartments, but Miss Mattie says, "I don't need it, Gloria. I can get along without it."

"I can't let you—" Aunt Glo starts.

But Miss Mattie reassures her, "You'd do the same for me," and she dabs at the ring her glass of tea left on the table.

I know that Miss Mattie lives on a tiny pension. And no matter how many pockets Aunt Glo searches, she's not gonna find a spare forty anywhere. So I cut into my savings to pay her back. It's worth forty dollars to know Constance is gone. For the time being, anyway.

WHEN AUNT GLO'S AT WORK, I'm in charge of Daphne, and it's too much, really, to be with her all the time. Sometimes I have to use the bathroom, and I don't want Daphne with me then.

So I find ways of keeping an eye on her—or an ear—when I'm in another part of the house. I tell her to practice her karaoke, and I hook up the machine, and she sings for an hour or two while I sit at the table and catch up on my homework. I have to turn in every assignment I missed—it's part of the deal I made with the principal—but I'm almost through the backlog.

Then I hook up Daphne's dance game, and she practices dance steps, following the arrows on the TV and leaping around on her little mat. The TV beeps whenever she misses a step, and she hollers out, "Damn!" and starts over, so I know she's still inside, still safe, even if I'm in the next room folding flyers and addressing envelopes for this weird woman who wants our county to invest in a special water filtration system. (She's paying me twenty cents an envelope to stuff her memo inside and address it, and I can do that while I watch TV. When I'm done, it'll be more than a hundred bucks.)

Dino Honeycutt might have given the school the money to buy a new camera, but I'm still paying him back. He doesn't know it yet—nobody does—but I'm still paying him back.

I SHOW MS. BRADY THE PICTURES I've taken at the Tech Center. Some of them she likes, but some of them she doesn't. She wants me to show energy, show emotion, show conflict in my pictures. She doesn't like the posed shots, not even of my automotive repair teacher and the girls.

"Memories aren't posed," she says. "The yearbook is a book of memories."

So I go back and snap emotion: the boy who's dropped a wrench on his toe, the others around him pointing and laughing.

"That's it," Ms. Brady says. "We'll keep that one for your portfolio." She tells me not to hurry my pictures—that sometimes it's best to wait.

"But what if I miss a good one?" I ask.

"So what?" she says. "Another chance will come."

It seems contradictory—that I should take my time and wait, and also that I should capture conflict and emotion. How can I do both? I ask Ms. Brady about it, and she says, "Live with the contradiction." Doesn't that sound just like somebody named Saraswati? I remember my dream of her at the carnival grounds in her bumper car going nowhere, driving into the wall. But maybe there's always a wall. Maybe Ms. Brady knows that and doesn't fight against it.

She makes a file on the computer for my best pictures. She titles it "Kendra Lugo," but I don't ask her to change it. We add in the picture of the rental lady's mother's feet, stretched into a patch of sunshine.

IT'S DECEMBER, AND ME and Daphne walk along the beach and look for splatterpoos at the water's edge. I don't know if they're plants or animals. They look like thin little leopard-skin jellies, brown-speckled, but with irregular shapes, oblong and wiggly, and they have tails that might be pieces of seaweed they've claimed.

Daphne jiggles them, says "Gross," picks them up with

sticks, and watches them drool back down toward the sand. She thinks they might be dolphin poop, but I'm pretty sure she's wrong. I don't know what they are, maybe a fungus, but I've seen them before, last winter and the winter before. Every year in the springtime, I forget about splatterpoos, and when I see them again, I think, *Oh yeah . . .*

That's the way it is with a lot of things. Clara Tinsley and Rhonda—I forget about them sometimes, and then I remember and think, *Oh yeah.*

I forget about Constance, who might stay in Florida for all eternity, or who might hitch her way back to the migrant camp one day and make her living picking tomatoes five miles down the road.

I forget sometimes that Daphne might be in danger. I forget sometimes that the danger might not even be Constance. It might be a boy who plays with oranges—or a girl like me who's still little and thinks she has cancer and needs a mouth to pull her nipples back out.

The splatterpoos blend in with the seaweed, so if you're not careful, you can step in them and slide. I don't know if it hurts them. I'm not sure if they're dead or alive.

If they're alive, and if I step in them, smear them into the sand, am I guilty? My daddy still swears he didn't know about the drugs stashed in the drawers of those bedroom suites. He says he was just moving furniture. But prison is full of people who claim their innocence. I wonder sometimes if Rhonda feels innocent or guilty. There must be days when she feels responsible for pushing open Jarvis Stanley's window and climbing into his house. Even if she thought she was innocent, she must see that he feels innocent, too.

Since I know that in the wintertime, splatterpoos wash up on the beach, is it my job to always remember, forever in December, to step careful?

ALL WEEK SNEAKY LOOKS AT ME AND GRINS. She catches my eye over the mashed potatoes and winks. One night after supper she pulls me into the bathroom and says, "You want to?"

"I don't know," I say.

"Just for fun," Sneaky says. "Come on. My momma's going out of town tomorrow night, and Tim-Tim's staying over." She sits right down to pee, with me in there with her, and I look away, even though part of me wants to see her legs.

"Tim-Tim'll be there?"

"Well, yeah," Sneaky says. "But he just wants to watch."

"No way," I say. "He's like my brother."

"Not really," she says. Then "Whoa." The downstairs pot's real wobbly, and when you lean over to get some toilet paper, you almost topple.

"That'd be incest," I say.

"No, it wouldn't," she says. "He's not really your brother. And besides that, he'd just be watching. I promise." She flushes and stands up real slow and takes her time pulling up her panties. I don't know why she does that to me. I can't help looking, but I turn away quick. I try to think about her eyes and not her private parts. She paints her eyes like a cat, with eyeliner on top, and I like how it looks.

"Come on," she says. "It'll be fun!" She buttons her jeans and then surprises me when she pulls up her shirt real quick and flashes her titties. She laughs and says, "Tim-Tim wishes they were bigger, but I just tell him that more than a mouthful's a waste."

I don't even know what to do with Sneaky. I watch her in the mirror and kind of smile, because what do you do with a girl like Sneaky?

"I'll get you some wine coolers," she offers. She's such a cute girl, too. She's got this tiny little nose that turns up at the tip.

I don't know what to say. I feel trembly in my legs, but not trembly-scared. I think about Ms. Brady and how she says not to rush when I'm taking pictures, that if I miss a good shot, others will come along, so I say, "Don't take this the wrong way, Sneaky. I like you and everything—but maybe when I'm eighteen..."

"Eighteen?" she asks and laughs. "Kenny, you're crazy. How come?" I shrug. It seems like I should be eighteen to make a big decision like that. "You are *too* cute," she says, and she gives me a squeeze. "When's your birthday?"

"March," I tell her. "Come on."

Aunt Glo's got a smear from a splatterpoo on a microscope slide, and I really want to see it.

J ARVIS STANLEY'S BEEN BADGERING ME ever since I put up my signs about doing odd jobs, telling me to come over when I get a chance. He's sent messages through Aunt Glo and Quincy both. "Tell that gal I need to see her," he says.

I know he wants me to come clean up his house, and I don't intend to do it. I don't intend to scrape what's left of Clara Tinsley's brains off the sides of the wall with a putty knife. I've heard how brains dry to cement, and that's not a job I'm doing, not for a hundred dollars an hour.

Though it's tempting. Not the job but the hundred dollars an hour, because Aunt Glo's microscope has a scratched-up lens. Whenever she looks at anything through the 10X, there's a black scraggly worm in the middle that we have to ignore. She's tried to clean it, but it's not dirt. It's permanent. If I had all the money in the world, I'd pay back Dino Honeycutt (I'm getting close to having enough for that), and I'd replace Aunt Glo's microscope, and I'd pay an electrician to finish the workshop, maybe even put a new roof on it.

I tell Aunt Glo, "If I had all the money in the world, I'd get you that security system."

It occurs to me that a security system would be a good thing in a lot of ways, for everybody involved. If Jarvis Stanley'd had a security system, it would have gone off as soon as Clara and Rhonda opened that window. And they wouldn't have climbed inside, not with all that beeping. And Jarvis wouldn't have needed to shoot the intruder, because there wouldn't have *been* an intruder. A security system would have given everybody a chance to make a better choice.

"Oh, honey," Aunt Glo says, "that's sweet of you."

But she's not really listening. She's copying a poem out of

a book to send to my daddy. She prints each word so careful, taking her sweet time.

"Seriously," I say. Then I tell her, "If I can stay here after I turn eighteen and get a job, then I can pay you rent, and you can use the money to get a security system. You won't ever have to worry about Constance again."

It seems like a great idea to me. So I'm not expecting it when Aunt Glo replies, "Some days I wish Constance wanted Daphne enough to try and steal her."

AFTER I GET PAID FOR STUFFING and addressing the envelopes and add in what I earned from Dino Honeycutt and from the Baptist preacher, I make a trip to the Coming Soon Luxury Condos. Fredo's working at that job site now, but there's no sign of Juan. For all I know, he could have run off to Florida with Constance. I wait until Dino shows up, and I meet him at his truck door.

"Hello, sir," I say, and I offer him my hand.

"Kenny," he says. "Good to see you." But he looks confused and a little worried. "How's school?" he asks, and I can tell that he thinks I've dropped out again.

"Just fine, sir," I say. "I brought you this."

I give him the money for the camera—two hundred and forty-nine dollars and sixty-seven cents, the exact amount the camera cost. (I found the receipt in the box.) I've got it sealed up in an envelope along with a copy of the receipt. "I appreciate what you did for me," I say. "But it's important to me to pay for that camera myself."

Dino nods, folds the envelope in half, and sticks it in his back pocket. "Come on," he says. "Let me show you what we're doing here," and then he gives me a tour of the job site. He opens up the plans for the buildings right on the hood of his truck, and he holds down one side while I hold down the other, and he shows me the different units, the designs for the outside of the building and the designs for the inside. He shows me the way the plumbing runs and the wiring. He points out the little roof decks that'll go on the top of each unit. From up there, the residents will have a view of the harbor.

"That's really something," I tell him. I know those condos will cost a fortune, but if I had all the money in the world, I might buy a condo and a telescope and sit on my roof deck and look at the stars.

"I'm gonna need somebody to help me manage this place," he says. "You graduate in June, don't you? That'll be just about the right time, and I could use somebody like you."

My heart's a bomb, booming in my toes, because I *should* be graduating, but I'm a year behind.

"I'm sorry, sir," I tell him. "I'm only a junior."

"Oh," he says. "I thought Wendy told me you were a year older than her."

"I am," I say. "But there was this one year when I was too sick to go to school." For the first time, I realize it's not exactly a lie. I *was* too sick, even if what I was sick about was imaginary.

It occurs to me that maybe I can get Aunt Glo on with

Dino Honeycutt, and then she'll be able to pay the high taxes and won't have to give up her family home at 206B Osprey Lane.

"I know just the person for that job, though," I say. "My Aunt Glo. She'd make a great manager, and I could help her out on weekends, and when I graduate, I can be your handyman."

"My handyman, eh?" he asks and laughs.

"Yes, sir," I say, and I list all the skills I already have.

He reaches into his wallet and pulls out his business card, two of them, and he says, "I may just take you up on that, Kenny. Give the other one to your aunt and have her call me." Then he rolls up his blueprints and wanders off to check on the foundation.

I'M WORKING IN THE WORKSHOP AGAIN, cutting pieces of thin molding for the edges of the floor, when something blocks out my light. I put down my handsaw and turn around to see Jarvis Stanley leaning in the doorway. It gives me a shiver to see him there.

"I'll say one thing for you," Jarvis says. "You don't never stop. Ain't never seen nobody work all the time like you do." I stand up, brush off my knees, and hold myself up as tall as I can, but already I'm feeling that hot flush rising in my face.

"Keeps you off the streets, I reckon," he says. "You got a miter box?"

"No, sir."

He nods toward my molding and says, "You'll make those cuts a lot better with a miter box. I got one you can borry." I don't even know how a miter box works, but I know about miter saws and wish I had one.

"See here," he says, "I've got a job I need done," and in my head I'm thinking *No, no, no,* but I feel like a caught fish, held up by a hook and flapping either way, 'cause how can I tell a neighbor (and Aunt Glo's friend) that I won't clean his house?

He doesn't ask me to clean after all. He needs me to climb up into his attic and get down his winter clothes. He's got a rope strung up there, and he swaps out his clothes every season. But last month he threw out his back, and he can't climb the attic stairs. So he's still wearing T-shirts and a lightweight jacket that's no good against the sharp winds that blow in off the bay.

Even though I ordinarily work out a price before I do a job, I don't discuss money with Jarvis. I tell him that I'll do it and ask him if I can come over in half an hour, since I want to tack down these pieces of molding first.

"Sounds good," he says. I wait for him to leave, but he doesn't. He looks around the workshop, inspects the floor, toes at the tiles, and nods.

"You've done a good job fixing this place up."

"Thanks," I say.

"Gloria told me it's gonna be your photography studio."

That catches me off guard. 'Cause I haven't talked about it with Aunt Glo at all. "She did?" I ask.

"So I reckon you probably gonna need this," he says. He reaches into his pocket and pulls out the camera—the first one, the one that Constance stole, except she didn't. "I been trying to give this back to you," he says. "I told Gloria to send you over. Reckon you didn't get the message."

"Where'd you get it?" I ask.

"Found it on the porch," he says. "That day the storm come. Yall'd gone to see your daddy, and I didn't want it to get wet."

I thought for sure I left it in the workshop. I know I left it in the workshop.

"Why didn't you tell me?" I ask.

"Tried to," he says. "But you been mighty busy. Too busy to hear."

I take the camera from him, the cold silver box, and I say, "Thank you," even though I'm still not sure he's telling the truth. Because maybe he stole it. Maybe he came into the workshop after we left and found it.

I turn it on, and the batteries still work. I hit the review button, and it still has the pictures I took.

I'd forgotten that the last picture wasn't of the workshop at all. It was a picture of the porch swing, taken down off its chains so it wouldn't blow into the house. The one before that was a picture of Sneaky and Tim-Tim in front of the van. (Posed. No good.) The pictures of the workshop came before that, then the pictures from the bus, the boy with his hand in front of his face, Sudie Montgomery's legs and book bag, then pictures from the Tech Center.

I'd forgotten.

I worked it all out in my head. I thought the camera was in the workshop and would have sworn to my story and blamed Constance till the end of time. But here it is: the camera, the picture I took of the porch swing.

Constance didn't steal it, but deep inside I know she would

have if I'd left it in the workshop. She'd have taken my camera to a pawnshop and used the money to buy a bus ticket to Miami.

Constance stole from me all right, but what she took wasn't a camera. She robbed me of the fantasy that Daphne belonged to me. She took security that wasn't really mine in the first place.

So I was wrong (and not wrong) to accuse her.

IT ONLY TAKES A COUPLE OF HOURS to move Jarvis's clothes: down to up, up to down. Daphne helps. She picks up the ones that fall off the hangers and helps me organize them in his closet, pants together, shirts together, coats together.

"All your clothes smell like used-up vacuum-cleaner bags," Daphne complains.

"Well, then, I reckon I better wash 'em," Jarvis says.

Every now and then Jarvis tries to grab Daphne and tickle her, but she wiggles away, and I'm right there, so if she ever doesn't, I'll knock him in the head with whatever's close by. Old pervert.

I wouldn't really have to do that, though. He's too slow and hobbles everywhere he goes. He leans on his cane and rubs his back. Daphne could get away by herself.

"Don't you wanna come be my little girl?" he asks Daphne.

"Shit, no," she says. "I got a home already."

I try to keep Daphne within arm's reach, but she's the one

who sneaks off into the living room to see if she can find any bloodstains on the floor. She's down on her hands and knees looking for bloodstains when we get in there. "Where'd it happen?" she asks.

"Right over there somewhere," Jarvis says.

"Do you get bad dreams about it?" Daphne asks him.

"Sometimes," he admits.

"Me, too," she says.

"Me, three," I add, and then we all just stand there in the stale quiet.

I try not to look around the living room too much. I want to, and then again I don't. It's kind of like watching Sneaky in the bathroom—I take little peeks and wonder if the slipcover on the couch is new or if it's been there forever.

Jarvis pulls out his wallet, an old leather one like my daddy used to tote. It's got a picture of a hunting dog engraved into the leather. I haven't seen one of those in a long time. I used to love to look at the picture on my daddy's wallet, and I wish for a minute I could hold Jarvis's, but I can't, of course.

He gives me a ten and Daphne a five.

"Why does she get more than me?" Daphne asks.

"'Cause she's older and works harder," Jarvis says, and he tries to cuddle with Daphne again, but I pull her away.

The lamp shade's definitely new. There's a sticker on the side telling what he paid for it at Wal-Mart. On the coffee table beside it, I see something that twists my guts in ways I can't explain: the picture of Clara Tinsley, cut out of the newspaper and put into a frame. It doesn't exactly fit—the frame's too big, too shiny, and it seems crazy for Clara to be there, grainy smiling Clara, right next to Jarvis's toenail clippers, his pouch of chewing tobacco, his highball glass with its amber residue edging the bottom.

Jarvis sees me looking. Maybe I blush or maybe I blanch, because he says, "You know, I hate it." He rubs his hand up and down his spine. "I wish like hell it hadn't happened."

S OMEONE WHISPERS MY NAME in the dark: "Kenny?"

It scares me because it happens so fast. I scramble awake, say, "Yeah?" and by then I've figured out it's Sneaky. "What's the matter?" I ask her, leaning over the bunk-bed railing. She's right beside the bed. She's come all the way into the room, and I didn't even hear her.

"I gotta talk to you," she says. "Can I climb up?"

But we'd wake Daphne for sure, so I come down. As I'm feeling around the floor for my jeans and yesterday's shirt, I'm thinking about Rhonda and Clara Tinsley, how, when Jarvis woke up, they were already *there*. I try to be quiet as I follow Sneaky down, but the stairs groan and screech, and I wonder if Jarvis can hear it through the walls and if my footsteps march right into his dreams and lead him back to the night he killed an almost innocent girl.

If I'd thought Sneaky was somebody coming for Daphne, and if I'd had a gun, I'd have shot her, too. Even if she wasn't really coming for Daphne.

"I gotta talk to you," Sneaky says again.

"Not here," I say. Because what if somebody has a gun, somebody who's dreaming?

I collect my shoes from the back door, my jacket from one of the kitchen chairs, and me and Sneaky head down to the beach. It's cold, but when I put my hands in my pockets for my gloves, I feel the camera there instead. The first one.

"I found a ring," Sneaky tells me. "I went snooping while Tim-Tim was getting a shower, and I found it."

"Where?" I ask.

"In a velvet box in his dungaree drawer," she says. "Can you believe it?" And she squeals.

"Shhh," I say.

"He's gonna ask me to marry him. What should I do?"

"I don't know," I tell her. "Are you sure?"

"There's nobody else for him to give a ring to, is there?" I love it that Sneaky's so confident. I'd never believe a ring I found was meant for me, not even if it had my name engraved on it.

Sneaky's got a blanket draped over her head and shoulders, clutched around her throat. It's a thin blanket, the one I put over Rhonda's legs that night she sat on our couch almost three months ago. I don't know if anybody's washed it since. I don't know where Sneaky's coat is, or why she's wearing a blanket like she's Little Red Riding Hood.

"Well, don't you get it?" Sneaky says. "This is our very last chance."

"For what?" I ask.

"Mine and yours. If Tim-Tim proposes to me, and I say yes, then I can't never have sex with anybody else," she explains. "Long as I live. So this is our last chance."

I can't believe Sneaky—one minute she's my friend, and

the next minute she's trying to get me in the sack. I can't help being pleased, even if I'm flustered.

"Even if he asks you, you don't have to say yes," I tell her.

"Well, I *do,*" she says. "If he asks me."

We're almost to the beach by then, past all the houses, so it's not like anybody's going to hear when I say, "Holy shit, Sneaky. You don't have to marry the first man that proposes!"

It makes my head spin, because Sneaky's the cutest girl ever, in all the world. But she's Tim-Tim's girlfriend, and she might turn into Tim-Tim's wife. And here she is tempting me again without even giving me the time to figure out my moves.

We cross over the dunes and tromp down onto the beach, and Sneaky slides her hand up under my shirt and tickles.

"No!" I say. "I can't."

"Why not?" she demands. She throws both hands up in the air and lets the blanket fall down around her.

"Wouldn't be right to sneak behind Tim-Tim's back."

Sneaky looks up at the moon and says, "Jesus! You couldn't do it with him looking, and now you can't do it in secret?" She pouts up her face like a little kid, and it's all I can do not to grab her and hug her.

I tell myself, *Don't grab her, don't hug her.* I'm thankful that it's, the middle of the night and my breath is a little bit sour, because I might grab her and hug her if circumstances were different.

"He wouldn't show you the same respect. I'll tell you that," Sneaky says. Then she picks up her blanket, turns, and runs down the beach. Her blanket follows behind like a parachute.

"Wait," I call, because I don't want her to be upset. "Sneaky, wait."

But she doesn't stop right away. She's running along the water's edge, and she doesn't stop until she trips. I'm right behind, but not close enough to catch her, and down she goes, somersaulting over something that turns out to be a big dead fish.

It's just the skeleton, really, a huge soft head, empty eye sockets, white bones, and strips of skin maybe two feet long. Probably somebody caught it, filleted it right on the boat, and then tossed the carcass to the gulls. That happens a lot. \

It's so common it wouldn't even be scary in daylight, but Sneaky hollers out, "Ugh!" and pulls herself up onto dry sand.

"It's all right," I tell her. But I'm laughing, I can't help laughing, and that pisses her off more.

"Ugh," she says again, half crying and brushing herself off. "I hate fish," she says. Then: "Damn you, Kenny. Shut up!"

The more she laments, the funnier it gets, so I flop down on the sand beside her. Pretty soon we're both conked out on our backs in the sand and laughing. "That's nasty!" she says, and she kicks sand with her feet like she's trying to bury that fish from afar.

"Not really," I say. I take in a big breath of briny beach air. "It doesn't even stink."

"Does, too," Sneaky argues, but there's no smell, not yet. Maybe a dog could smell it, but not a person. "Looks like something out of a horror movie."

"But it's not," I tell her. "It's just an ordinary red drum. A *grown* one, though."

"Don't look ordinary to me," she says.

So I lean forward and grab what's left of the fish by the tail.

"Don't touch it!" Sneaky says, but it's too late. I drag it closer to where we're sitting.

"This kind of fish is an old homebody," I tell her. "Did you know that? Red drum spend their whole lives in the same place they're born. This fish has probably lived here longer than Aunt Glo."

"No way," Sneaky says.

"Sure," I tell her. "They can live fifty years, maybe more."

"Kinda sad it got caught, then," Sneaky observes, and I agree. You'd think after that many years, it'd know to avoid the bait.

It's the strangest feeling, sitting out there on the sand with Sneaky while, back home, Tim-Tim snores in his bed. "I want to ask you something," I say.

"What?"

"Do you want to be with me—that way—just to experiment? Or do you really like me?"

"Kenny," she says. "Of course I like you." But I can tell by her tone that she's squirming in her heart.

"No," I say. "Tell the truth."

"It started out as an experiment," Sneaky admits. "I mean, I've never been with a woman before."

"Most girls haven't," I say.

"But why not?" Sneaky says. "I mean, really! If Reba McEntire came up to me tomorrow and wanted to be my lover, how could I say no? I'd run right off with her!"

That strikes me funny, picturing Sneaky and Reba on the country-music circuit.

"Really!" Sneaky says. "But then I figured you'd like it, too. I mean, look at this body! How could you pass this up?" and she holds her arms out to the sides.

I look, of course. I've looked a hundred times.

"I thought it'd do you good, too," Sneaky says. "Don't look to me like you enjoy your body very much. So I just thought you might wanna enjoy mine." She raises her eyebrows at me and shrugs.

"So I'm a charity case?"

"That's not what I meant."

In the moonlight, what's left of the fish seems so white, unnaturally white, almost glowing. Up close you can tell that this fish was caught by fishermen, because the head's intact (except for the eyeballs). If a shark had gotten it, the head would've been eaten, too. Up close, you can see remnants of meat along the bones. The knife knew just how to sliver and saw the meat away from the skeleton.

I pick up a strip of skin, coated with sand and twisting on itself, and again Sneaky says, "Ugh." I like her disgust. Part of me wants to disgust her. I pull the strip away from the carcass.

"These scales," I say. "They're big and hard. You can tell they come off the back of the fish because they're so rough. On the underside, on the breast, the scales are smooth and littler."

I can't help thinking about Sneaky's breasts, small and smooth, and my own beneath my bandages, big and rough with scabs from the lack of air. Your skin needs air on it if you're a person. If you're a fish, it's the very worst thing.

Suddenly I want to take a picture of this fish. Down the beach about a hundred yards, there's the pier. It's lit from the underside, and I'll need the light to get a halfway decent shot.

"Come on," I tell Sneaky, and we get up, and I grab the fish by the gills, just like I'd caught it, and I walk down the beach dragging the carcass.

"You're the only person in the world who'd ever want a

picture of a decomposing fish, Kenny," Sneaky says.

"Maybe so," I say.

"You're not a charity case," she tells me as we walk. "You're different from anybody else I've ever met."

"You mean I'm gender-confused," I say. It's a term I heard Aunt Glo use on the telephone with Daddy a long time ago, and it seems to me the kindest way to say it.

"No," Sneaky says. "I mean you're like a boy in all the good ways, and you're kind of like a girl in all the good ways, too." She pauses and then adds, "Except you need to let your boobies out to breathe."

And I think: *Maybe when I'm eighteen.*

I don't want Sneaky to see me smile, so I don't look back. I set the fish on a rock near the pier, climb up, and then move the carcass to a higher rock, nearer to the light.

"You see things other people don't see," Sneaky says.

I arrange the fish and flip through the dial on the camera until I come to the one for night shots, and I take a picture. But in that weak light, it's impossible to judge the quality.

So I pick up the fish to move it again, and Sneaky says, "I want a picture of you with that fish."

"No," I say. "I don't let people take my picture."

"Come on," she says. "I don't have any pictures of you."

"That's the way I like it," I say, but in the end she talks me into it. She says she wants to capture the night we almost made love.

"But we didn't," I say.

"But we could have," she tells me.

So I hold up the fish like I've just pulled it in, except there's nothing but head and vertebrae dangling down. It might not be a red drum at all. I can't really tell. It might be a cobia, a black drum, something else. I hold it up proud, and I smile for Sneaky. Then I hold it like a baby, curling its big dead head in the nook of my arm, cradling its bones in the other.

Sneaky says, "Ugh!" and laughs and clicks.

I let her take a dozen.

WE'VE COME OUT HERE TO FISH, me and Quincy and Daphne and Aunt Glo and Tim-Tim and Sneaky. It's December, but there's no wind today. The bay's quiet, completely flat. A single piece of pine straw floats around the place where my fishing line enters the water, and I watch it, and it almost puts me to sleep.

We heard that the stripers were out, but they must be deep. They're not biting here, not from the pier, and in a while Quincy gives up and crawls down on the rocks that jut out into the water. His hair falls long into his face. I watch him in the distance, trying to catch sea roaches and fish with his hands. He's got on gloves without fingers, and I know the gloves are already wet.

Aunt Glo wears a scarf over her head to cover her ears. She looks like a movie star, sitting behind her sunglasses with her face turned up and warming there. I can't tell if she's awake or not.

Tim-Tim holds Daphne upside down off the pier and

pretends like he's gonna drop her. She hollers and howls. Her pink coat bells down over her head, and her shirt rides up, exposing her jiggly belly. Sneaky says, "Baby, be careful!" Daphne's laughing, but maybe she's scared, too. I can't protect her from everything. Not from her uncle, who's only playing. But if he drops her, I'll dive right in. I hope I can swim good enough to save her.

If I have to dive in, then I'll dive. I'll do what I have to do, or what I think I have to do.

"Stop!" Daphne hollers when something plinks into the bay. It's one of her plastic bracelets, yellow and pink beads on a stretchy elastic cord. She's mad at Tim-Tim, who apologizes as he sets her down red-faced on the wooden boards and says, "I'll buy you another one." She rams him in the stomach with her head, then comes over to me and asks me to dive in and get it for her.

"No way," I say.

"If you loved me, you would," she pouts.

"Make Tim-Tim get it," I say. "He's the one who made you lose it."

But Tim-Tim's moved down the pier with Sneaky, and they smooch a time or two. Then Tim-Tim carves their names into the wood while Sneaky shows Aunt Glo her diamond again. It's a tiny chip of a diamond, but in the afternoon sun, it catches the light so pretty.

I catch a baby croaker, way too little to eat, and that distracts Daphne from her floating-away bracelet. I cut the fish into steaks, give one to Daphne, put one on my line, and chunk it into the bay, hoping to tempt the striper with something fresh.

"You *gotta* catch something now," Sneaky calls. "Now that you killed a baby fish for it!"

"Don't be so tenderhearted," Daphne calls back. "This is your supper!"

And so we fish. We fish and tease one another, but we don't catch anything big enough to keep.

"Well, I swannee," Aunt Glo says after a while. "Just yesterday in the paper, there was a column on the striper. Said they were catching 'em ten and twelve pounds apiece."

"Don't make good sense," Tim-Tim agrees. "Tide's falling. Wind's from the west."

According to everything we can figure, we should be tearing them up, but we're not.

"Maybe they all went to a wedding," Daphne says. "A fish wedding out there by the channel marker."

"Maybe so," I say. I spot her bracelet floating down the way, but I don't mention it because I'm not sure I can hook it.

"If I was a fish, that's where I'd get married," Daphne says, and she points out into the open water.

"Not me," I tell her. "If I was a fish, I'd get married over there across the harbor under that old rickety pier."

"That's an ugly place," Daphne says. "Must be a hundred years old."

"I like the shadows," I say. "And think of all the barnacles cousined up on those old pilings. I'd want the barnacle choir to sing at my wedding."

"Not me," Daphne says. "I'd want the sting ray choir."

"Hey, look what I caught," I say as I reel in Daphne's bracelet. The thing only cost a quarter to begin with; it came out of one of those candy machines in the front of the grocery store. But Daphne puts it on like it's a prize. She wraps it around her ring finger six or seven times, until her whole finger is covered in plastic beads and bay water, and she mocks Sneaky, holding out her hand so you can inspect her goods.

So we talk for a while about weddings. Sneaky's got a plan to attend all the different churches in town, and when she picks one with an aisle she likes, she's going to get saved there and join up, so they'll let her and Tim-Tim get married for free. "Needs a big aisle," she explains, "cause my daddy uses a wheelchair. So we need a lot of room so he can give me away."

We didn't even know Sneaky had a daddy, much less a paralyzed Alabama daddy, so we hear stories about him for a while.

I get sleepy in the sunshine, and I close my eyes and wrap the fishing line around my finger so I'll feel any tugs. I fish like the blind until Daphne calls me over. "I need you to do me a big favor," she says seriously.

"Another one?" I ask, but I'm already digging through the cooler for a hunk of squid, because I assume something's nibbled at her line and eaten off her bait. In context, that's the obvious favor.

"No," Daphne says. "I want you to give me away."

"What?"

"When I get married," she explains, "I want you to be the one who walks me down the aisle."

"Okay," I tell her, and she grins at me long and hard, showing all the stubs of teeth breaking crooked through her gums.

For a minute, I go blind looking at the white edges of her new teeth and the water just beyond, glittering so sharp in the sunshine that it fills my eyes with stars right there in the middle of the day. And everything inside me feels like it turns to liquid gold, warm and wet and thick and important. It's a wonder I can hug her, given how melted I am. Then I kiss her on top of the head real quick and turn back to my fishing before anybody notices.

It's a perfect day, in a way, except we don't catch a thing. In a little bit Aunt Glo hollers, "Look!"

She's the one who sees the dolphins first, not far from us at all. A fin breaks the water, a gray back that looks almost greased, then another. She points them out, and Sneaky and Daphne both squeal and run over to where I'm fishing, because I'm closest.

We huddle together and watch them, and I wonder if they're from the same family or if they met up somehow, out there in the bay.

"I bet those dolphins came for the striper wedding," Daphne says. She points to one and asks, "Is that a boy or a girl?" but nobody knows. You really can't tell. Not from where we're standing.

The dolphins swim in unison and look almost like one animal with lots of curves and fins. They don't splash at all and barely part the water in spite of being so big. When one comes up, it makes the quietest sound, like an exhaling. They say, "Shhhh," but Aunt Glo talks anyhow. "Oh, they're pretty," she says. "If I had a camera, I'd take a picture and send it to Greg."

I do have a camera. As a matter of fact, I have two—one that belongs to Ms. Brady and one that belongs to me, I guess, since I paid for it.

I dig a camera out of my pocket and take a picture. But there's a lag, and by the time the camera secures the image, the dolphins are submerged again. I hold the camera ready, and Tim-Tim says, "Now!" and I click the button. Daphne says, "Did you get it? Let me see."

But again and again, I get water.

"If you're gonna be our wedding photographer, you're gonna have to do better than that!" Tim-Tim jokes.

"I will," I tell him.

"You gonna take their wedding pictures, Kenny?" Aunt Glo asks, and I shrug, and Sneaky says, "Sure she is."

So we have all these pictures of the bay, and then some pictures of us, too, posing on the pier, and a picture of Quincy on his belly hanging off a rock. There are pictures of my face and Daphne's, of my face and Sneaky's, of my face and Aunt Glo's, distorted and smushed together, like fun-house people. They're posed, sure, but they're still memories. A different kind of memory.

W HEN OTHER PEOPLE LOOK at these pictures of us, they'll just see people playing with a camera on a regular old Sunday afternoon, limited by the lens, by the length of my arm as I tried to take each shot. When other people look at these pictures of the bay, they'll just see water. Water and more water.

But I'll know there's a dolphin down there somewhere. I'll know there's a striper, married to a red drum, carrying on with oysters and all the bottom feeders. There's a dolphin down there somewhere in a world as real as ours, just beyond the things that we can see.

About THE AUTHOR

SHERI REYNOLDS is the *New York Times* bestselling author of five novels, including *The Rapture of Canaan*. She lives in Virginia and teaches at Old Dominion University,where she is the Ruth and Perry Morgan Chair of Southern Literature.

Available October 2012

the
HOMESPUN WISDOM
of MYRTLE T. CRIBB

A NOVEL

SHERI REYNOLDS

1

What I did was no more interesting or sinful than this: I took a handful of my husband, Craig's, back pain pills with me when I left that morning for my little operation because I was worried about the potential for pain later in the day. I worried that the doctor might tell me to take ibuprofen—because male doctors often do that to females, refuse to prescribe for them what they'd automatically prescribe for a man; some of them don't even realize they're still blaming Eve—and I didn't want to suffer on my drive back home or into the night. So I took a handful of Craig's medicine as a simple precaution.

My nerves were kinked and frazzled. I'd been up most of the night worrying, and to complicate things more, the fog that morning was so thick you couldn't see, the kind of fog we refer to around here as a malignancy of air. My side mirrors were clouded and wet, and my rearview mirror was broken, so I could barely see to back out of the driveway. Back then I drove Craig's old green truck with the camper top on it. The rearview mirror had been gone for so long that when

Craig had taken the truck in for its yearly inspection, he'd had to bribe the fellow to give us a sticker with some fresh flounder he'd caught that day. So, backing out of the driveway, I rolled down the window, stuck my head out as best as I could, and said a prayer that anything with sense enough to hear the tires crunching on the crushed up clam shells would stay out of my way.

Fog can confuse you because everything looks like an x-ray of itself, recognizable but not reliably so. As I made my way up the road, I gripped the wheel harder than I needed to, feeling not quite like myself. I worried about Craig out there on his boat. The crabbing season had just started up, but how would they even be able to find their crab pots in that weather? Depending on visibility, he might have to come back in, or maybe he was still in the harbor, waiting out the fog. And wouldn't it be just my luck if he decided to swing by the school to bring me flowers (something he's never done) and discover that I'd taken off for the doctor's appointment I'd kept a secret from him?

So I was anxious, naturally, and I caught myself gulping air by accident. I didn't want to have gas by the time I got to the doctor, especially considering the region of my body where he'd be working. That's when I decided to take one of Craig's pain pills—to relax my muscles and calm my nerves, offsetting any potential pain, and also, hopefully, preventing the pootsies.

I don't know if you can blame the drugs for what happened next. My appointment was a two-hour drive away, scheduled for eleven, so I had plenty of time to think. But as I got closer to the doctor's office, the truck started slowing down. It seemed like my foot didn't have the power to push that gas pedal hard enough to get me there on time. I started second-guessing myself, thinking that if I was going to spend my entire secret savings, it should be on something I looked forward to, maybe a trip with my girlfriend Dottie to Atlantic City to play the slot machines or to Pigeon Forge, Tennessee, where Dolly Parton sings.

With Craig's medicine in me, loosening me up, I started wondering if I should be getting my procedure done at all. It was elective surgery and wouldn't have been covered by my insurance even if I'd been fool enough to show them my benefits card. Of course, then the Human Resources supervisor at the elementary school where I work might find out what Craig had been teasing me about for years: I'm lopsided down there, between my legs, with one regular-sized lip and the other one pouting over it. Craig used to make jokes. Sometimes he'd accuse me of attempting to sprout a little ding-a-ling of my own. Sometimes when I'd get out of the shower, he'd point and laugh until I hopped into my panties. "For Lord's sake, baby," he'd say. "Can't you roll that thing up and tuck it somewhere?"

Now where was I supposed to tuck it?

(If it makes you squirm to read this, take a deep breath and hang in there. There are women all over creation ashamed of their bodies, and we need to talk about it more than we do.)

To his credit, Craig always ended such conversations

saying things like, "I'm just messing with you, baby. Don't sulk," or else he'd bring me home a milkshake to make up. But I lived with that kind of teasing day in and day out, and ultimately, it was what drove me toward my spiritual awakening. Right there on that highway headed north, I got just as gnarly-hearted as I could be. What right did Craig have to make me feel bad about my biology? I didn't pick my coochie size any more than I picked my eye color. I got mad with that doctor who'd sworn I'd be happier when I was *symmetrical*, showing me pictures of other women who looked like little girls and making me think I wanted to look that way, too.

And I got aggravated with myself for being suckered by them both. I got so mad that when I stopped to fill up the gas tank, I bought myself a Slurpee—a big one (I wasn't supposed to have anything to eat or drink before my procedure), and I took *another* one of those pills, this time *just because I could*.

I drove right past that doctor's office, blowing the horn and shooting the bird at somebody in the parking lot. (That's not something I'm proud of, and I only tell you this to demonstrate the degree of my frustration. That poor woman was probably there to have her clitoris dehooded, bless her bones.) At that point, I didn't know where I was headed. I just knew that wherever it was, I was going to have my oversized lippy when I got there.

So these were the conditions that led me to the place where I am today, and here are some things to consider, if you ever find yourself in similar straits.

MEATY TIDBITS

Your body isn't a topiary garden. There's nothing wrong with one body part being shaped differently than another. If your husband, wife, or otherwise beloved gives you grief about your symmetry, send that person out into the natural world. Look at the trees growing in your yard or neighborhood. Trees don't grow symmetrically. They stretch and branch and sometimes even contort themselves. The only trees and bushes that look perfectly symmetrical are owned by neurotics with hedge trimmers. These people are akin to plastic surgeons, and you'd do well to stay away from them.

If trees and plants aren't proof enough, have a look at the birds. Go sit on your porch and watch the little finches that make nests in your hanging fern and keep you from being able to take it down when it dies. If you can get a finch to stop hopping around long enough, you'll see that the feathers on either side don't match precisely. Watch the cat, sitting on the mailbox, hoping to grab the finch right out of the fern. The cat has one black paw when all the rest are tabby, and do you think that cat goes around ruminating and bellyaching about it? The cat knows it's perfect as it is. You're also perfect. So before you go looking for someone to balance your breasts, before you wear your hair in a strange configuration to hide your over-large ears, just remember: you could have bigger problems. You could be a finch with asymmetrical feathers, living in a half-dead fern, stalked by a cat with mismatched paws who won't give a fe-fi-fo-fum about your feathers when he crunches down on your tiny bones. Symmetry is overrated. Think about that before you go lopping off your own meaty tidbits.

Printed in the USA
CPSIA information can be obtained
at www.ICGtesting.com
JSHW022323140824
68134JS00019B/1255

9 781618 580337